CROSS RO

SEQUEL TO CROSS

To Grace and David :
You have visited this valley.

"Cross Road"—Huon Valley, Tasmania

THE MEMOIRS OF

MANAEN – THE PEASANT PASTOR

LUCILLE L. TURFREY

From Lucille with love.

ISBN: Hardcover   978-1-6641-0539-3
               Softcover   978-1-6641-0538-6
               eBook   978-1-6641-0537-9

Print information available on the last page.

Rev. date: 07/15/2021

To order additional copies of this book, contact:
Xlibris
AU TFN: 1 800 844 927 (Toll Free inside Australia)
AU Local: 0283 108 187 (+61 2 8310 8187 from outside Australia)
www.Xlibris.com.au
Orders@Xlibris.com.au
817259

CROSS ROADS

Cross Roads is the sequel to the historical novel titled *Cross Purposes* where Manaen, who grew up with Herod (see Acts 13:1), tells the Gospel story via his personal friendship with Jesus. In this, the sequel to *Cross Purposes* where he was introduced as "the Palace Peasant", Manaen now becomes "the Peasant Pastor" as he opens new windows on the Early Church. We will meet up with, and gain new perspectives on, many of its actual characters as they describe a "novel" means of constructing the building blocks of the New Testament.

In effect, *Cross Roads* may be viewed as an innovative approach to the New Testament's portrayal of the Early Church with the accompanying illuminating, factual background material adding to one's comprehension of the original text.

All paraphrased Scripture, all poetry/songs, all illustrations—paintings, sketches, and photography—are the work of the author and as such are subject to copyright restrictions. Some sketches have been used in prior publications, including *Contentment* by Keith Banks. (See page 4).

The poem *Hope* (see page 57), was inspired by a speech given by Winston Churchill in the early days of WWII. In the "Picture Parables" relating to the Hebrew Alphabet, the author has been guided by reference to various works including a *Hebrew Alphabet Chart* by W. B. Steele-Smith (circa 1946). Pages 218–222 provide the author's response to the Hebrew Alphabet—Ancient and Modern. Readers may enjoy working on the unused "Picture Parables", allowing the ancient Hebrew to reveal its stories as guided by those utilised in Manaen's class.

The Interlinear Bible—Hebrew/English (AP&A), *Beacon, IVP, William Barclay's Bible Commentaries* and *Young's Analytical Concordance* have been particularly useful.

The author is indebted to the proofreading skills of Mavis Smith, friend and colleague. The technical assistance of Phil McCorriston and Jenni Frost is also highly valued.

ACKNOWLEDGEMENTS

Illustrations by the author, located
on pages 1, 57, 98, 102, 164, 166, 201 in *Cross Purposes*
and 49, 86 in *Cross Roads* are reproduced
by kind permission of the General of
The Salvation Army. First published by Salvation Books,
The Salvation Army Headquarters, London,
in *Contentment*, a book of poems by Keith Banks
and illustrated by LLT.

...

Maryam's notes for the series on grief (see pages 91–103) are based
on a book by the author—*On a Winter's Mourning*—published by The
Salvation Army in Australia and used by permission.
The occasional songs/hymns/poems are similarly drawn mostly from
prior publications: *The Jesus Story in Song, St John's Psalms, Faith Alive*,
by the author, published by the Salvation Army in Australia and used
by permission, or written specifically for inclusion in *Cross Roads*.

All profits from royalties accrued from
Cross Purposes and its sequel, *Cross Roads*
will be donated to The Salvation Army's international
ministry among deprived children.

CROSS ROADS

THE ROUTE

1. THE NEW BEGINNING

'Maryam, *Mimi*, this is our family! We've come home! Here we are in a new country, a new people, a new language, a new faith. But we're home, Maryam, home!'

'Yes, dear heart, we are indeed. Much more than that, we are together. Oh, Manaen, I miss him so! David, gone from us. A stone, just one misguided rock—an assassin's stone—and our son is taken from us... But the Lord is so good. He has brought a peace to my heart. He met with David at the end. He took him "Home" to be with Him. Manaen, I know it now: death is not the end, it is a new beginning. I must learn more about what it means to have Eternal Life in the here and now, Manaen.'

'*Mimi*, joy of my heart, we will hold David's memory in our heart always and—in Heaven—there is a reunion awaiting us. There will be no final parting of the family *ben* Baruch! Come, dearest, we are to meet with our new "family" this morning. Saul—the transformed "Terror from Tarsus"—will come to escort us to the meeting house. I still can't get over it: the "Terror from Tarsus", a—what is it that they call themselves? *Christ-*ians! That's it! And Saul. He's been transformed. He's a new man, Maryam, a new man! He is a member of the Church. The Church! I must remember that the word has nothing to do with the building that has become the address where the Church—the Faith Community—meet. The Church is the people, not the building where they meet.'

Saul was right on time and took us quickly through the streets of Antioch to meet all those assigned to specific tasks of ministry for the people of their city. All rose in a welcoming way as Nicolas—who had aided us in our perilous escape from Jerusalem—Maryam and I entered the room.

We had just arrived in this Syrian city after our exit under the cloak of darkness through the western gate of Jerusalem. The trek westward, down through the mountains toward Joppa, had enabled us to board a ship bound for these Syrian shores.

Barnabas, whom I had known as Joseph when he visited all his relations in Jerusalem, took the floor. His task of today was to present us to the Christians of Antioch. 'Friends, I am pleased to introduce you to Nicolas, one of the "Serving Seven" in the Faith Community in Jerusalem. Nicolas is a "son of Antioch". He has come home! On the journey, he has given valuable service to his friends, Manaen and Maryam, whose story you will come to know in greater measure as time goes by.

'What will be of some surprise to you right now, I'm sure, is that Maryam is—in fact—a princess, belonging to the family of Herod Antipas. There was an excited chorus of "ooh and ah" as Barnabas continued. 'Be assured of this, Maryam has no wish to be treated in any special way for she has emphasised to me her deep desire to be entirely one of us! Maryam will wear no "crowns or coronets"!' Now some rowdy hand-clapping filled the room and Barnabas had need to give pause to the proceedings before continuing his introductions.

'Manaen—in his Hebrew language, *Menachem (the comforter)*—is the "Palace Peasant". Pardon me, Manaen, I could not resist the opportunity to comment on the fact that you grew up with Herod Antipas and his family in the palace of Herod the Great—the Herodion—just south of Bethlehem in Judea.

'We welcome you, Nicolas, Maryam and Manaen, into the Church! Please know that we look upon you already as being integral members of this "family". Yes, there's much work to do but you will find that it does not outweigh our depth of fellowship. We worship here. We witness here, and—at times— we fair bubble over with sheer joy as we recognise the many miracles occurring as we "trust and obey".

'We seek to do the Lord's will for this Church, the Faith Community. We are still getting to know, and be familiar with, these new terms but I think they suit us well. Let us now pray the prayer of thanksgiving and seek the Lord's blessing upon you each.' There followed a time of extempore prayer with many vocalising their praise and intercessions.

The key leaders of the local church were then introduced in turn—the prophets (the preachers): Barnabas, Simeon and also Lucius; then the teachers, of whom Saul held the prominent position. We discovered that young John Mark was also an assistant member of the group. Barnabas explained that there had been many gifts from this church—the Faith Community—that would enable the furnishing of our new *beth* (home). Then a jubilant chatter broke out and there was much by way of back-slapping and happy hugs! 'Please tell us about your palace days, Manaen.' 'Is that where you met Maryam?' 'Do tell us!' 'How did you manage to escape from Jerusalem?' Questions came fast and frankly. I answered each as best I could.

Barnabas brought Simeon across to meet with me, introducing him by his "pet" name, *Niger* (the "black man"). No! Never, no! I already know this man! 'It is so good to see you again, Simeon! How can I ever forget the first day of our meeting? You were closer than I to *Yeshua*–Jesus when He fell. How I would have longed to carry His cross-beam on that "death-march" to *Golgotha.* But you were there. You picked it up; you shouldered it. You found your faith on that blood-stained path as you walked with our Saviour to Calvary! You are truly more than my friend. You're my brother! Let's seal it with a grip of the hand!'

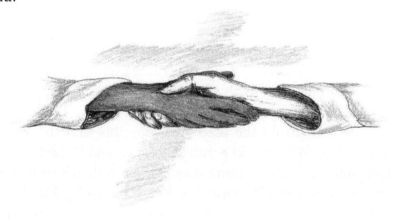

'Now, you must be Lucius,' I said, turning to a second man of like ilk. 'Your homeland is Libya, I understand. Two men of Africa, now brothers with the Christian family here in Antioch!'

At this point, Saul came across to join in the conversation. 'Ah, I see you three have met! Manaen, I may well be a teacher here at Antioch but I must say that the teacher is being taught! Lucius and Simeon have brought up close to me the deeper issues of human personality, goodness, Godliness, brotherhood where racism has no place, no affinity, no part of the in-look and out-look of the Christian Church. In fact, I am going to make this truth a central theme in my teaching everywhere!

'Manaen, Lucius, Simeon, what have you say of this bold statement? *We are all sons and daughters of God because of our faith in Jesus Christ. All who commit their lives to Him have been clothed in His righteousness. There are no Jews nor Greeks, there are no slaves nor masters, no men nor women, for we are all ONE in Christ Jesus. If you belong to Christ then you belong to the Family, you are heirs to the Kingdom of God.* (See Galatians 3:26–29)

'I'll refine the gist of what will become a kind of cornerstone, a foundation, on which I will preach in building up the world-wide Church. I would be glad of your considered reactions so that I can mould the message in a way that will hold no queries, no objections, no stumbling blocks to faith.'

'Saul,' I asked, 'what is so important about the different shades that are applied to the skin—the outer cladding of all that lies under its fragile form? We are all made of the same materials under the skin. The heart is not white or black, or any *diverse* colour in between. It throbs with rich red blood and, let us never forget, the life is in the blood! The skin would soon crumple into nothingness if the blood ceased sending its flow to our wrappings! And, with what colour can we paint the human soul? Such is not to be found on the palette of an artist. It is moulded into the texture of people who have been born again, a people made whole and holy; a people who are "coloured" by the Light of God, our Heavenly Father!'

We sat together informally, enjoying a fine luncheon. Stories were exchanged with happy banter intermingled with the deeper accounts of life-changing experiences. What a happy "family" this is! Maryam and I sought to discover as much as we could about Antioch, its importance as a major city, and how best we could settle into the ways, whys and wherefores of our new home.

We were informed that only Rome itself and Alexandria ranked higher than this Syrian city of Antioch! We had already discovered that it was here where the Faith Community was first referred to as Christian. It seemed to us that its citizens were prone to attach labels, in a fond sort of way, to people and places. Take Simeon, for example, the man labelled "Niger".

We came to realise that this location was ideal for the growth and development of the Christian Church. The rigid structures in which Judaism bound the believers in Jerusalem did not apply in Antioch where—as Saul put it so exceedingly well—there is neither Jew nor Greek for we are all ONE in *Yeshua*–Jesus!

The general assembly had finally departed and then the local leaders called us to a board room table where we took our seats to commence a business session. Following items of general concern, Barnabas spoke of some special plans that the Church was hoping to introduce. With the coming of Nicolas, a Syrian "Serving Seven" could be set in place here. The city was crying out for the poor to receive practical and spiritual help. Then, looking straight at me, Barnabas spoke of the need to set up a Christian *Akademeia*—Academy—named after *Akademos*, the hero after whom Plato's garden was named. He said, 'The Church is already blessed with some fine teachers but the Community as a whole are pleading for more teaching regarding the Heritage of The Faith. What of the Holy Writ? What does *YHVH, El Shaddai* (LORD, God the Almighty) require? What are our beginnings? How will the truths of the past enhance the verities of today? We need to act before this high level of inquiry dissipates.

'Manaen, we turn to you. Saul has informed us of your value as a teacher of great repute. He has observed you at close proximity and knows that you are the man that the Lord has prepared to undertake the role of Headmaster! Already, our students are almost battering down our doors in their hunger to be fed spiritually. What will you say?'

'I hardly know what to say!' 'That is a first for you, Manaen!' I knew the voice—it was the erstwhile "Terror from Tarsus"! We laughed. I took a deep breath that somehow included "Breath of God—the Holy Spirit of Pentecost" and I found myself able to say, 'I believe the Lord has prepared me for this time. All the years that have been before have been a preparation. All those years of "cross purposes" have been designed to consolidate in me the "purpose of The Cross". I do accept with heartfelt joy!'

The skills associated with teaching seemed to flow into my mind-set without too many traumas. I knew the privilege that was mine in being given the opportunity to open the pages of Holy Scripture to enquiring students who were intent on taking its truth into their own lives. I saw the earnest student as one who allowed "shapeless clay" to become moistened and made ready for the Lord's—the Potter's—hands.

The Potter at Work, Melbourne, Australia

Never the Potter, my role will be to bring the clay to the potter's wheel, to encourage the student to become malleable in the Potter's hands—conforming to the pattern that He desires.

The response to my acceptance of this tremendous privilege–cum–responsibility was heart-warming. 'Hallelujah! We rejoice with you.' 'You are God's man for the task!' 'It will not be easy.' 'You will need time to settle in.' 'We have a home prepared for you.' 'You need some space, also, to recuperate after that arduous journey of escape from Jerusalem.'

'Manaen, how will you begin?' I heard the question but could not tell its source. It was time for a light-hearted response. 'I will start at the very beginning! With an ox, a house, and a camel.'

'An ox?' 'A house??' 'A camel???' Everyone was amazed— some, aghast! Even Saul's mouth looked fit to drop! Then, the light dawned for him. His shock turned to pure joy. 'Of course! Of course! The very place to start! This is wonderful! Superb! I guarantee a remarkable commencement for the Christian Academy!'

Though the members were placated by Saul's affirmation, they could not determine any logical way in which an ox, a house and a camel would, in all the realms of possibility, commence the most serious and challenging study about to be undertaken by the students of the newly formed Christian Academy! Saul and I allowed them their mutterings: 'Well, the ox would be in the field.' 'But Manaen would be at home.' 'Preparing for a pilgrimage to Persia, no doubt.' 'Or, will he take his pupils on to Babylon?' 'Perhaps we had better turn up as students, learn just what there is to know of oxen, homes and camels!'

It was time to depart. Saul took charge of the new team members. He guided us to our new residence, certainly not to be compared with the marriage gift from Herod Antipas but so very homely. Already, the many gifts from the Faith Community were gracing our new abiding place. Saul took his leave of us, promising to return when we were ready to commence work.

We rested, together, on a comfortable seat and all but drifted off into somnolence. But not before we voiced our thankfulness to *YHVH El Shaddai*. 'Maryam, where is my writing kit? Before this day is done, we must compose a psalm of thankfulness. Let's share our thoughts as I make ready my parchment and the writing tools.'

As I took the case in hand, I recalled the poignancy of my *bar mitzvah* when my parents, Yehudith and Baruch, my Mother and Father—my *emi* and *abbi*—had presented me with my precious writing kit. The words began to form and we shared how best to fit the rhythm with the rhyme (no longer synchronized with Hebraic forms of poetry though the content fitted well with the Hebrew style of "agreement"—the second line agreeing with the first and so on through the psalm). I began to write:

GOD'S STEADFAST LOVE
(Choir: *Rimington* L.M.)

How steadfast is the love of God!
It does not change, it will abide;
God's loving-kindness does not cease,
We find Him in the heart's deep peace.

How constant is the grace of God,
Revealed within His precious word.
So undeserved yet bountiful,
It is through grace we are made whole.

How faithful are the ways of God!
He keeps His word, He IS: the Lord!
His promises remain secure
And through the ages will endure.

How lasting is our joy in God!
We walk by faith, we trust His word;
The Lord is our inheritance,
He is our hope, we're in His hands.

The steadfast love of God prevails,
His boundless mercy never fails;
It's new each morning! This our praise:
Great is Your faithfulness always!

It was more than time we took our rest. And, rest we did before the immediate challenges of our new life filled our waking thoughts.

2. THE ACADEMY

For two days, I sat in studious thought with my writing kit at the ready. As ideas came to mind, they were duly recorded. I was in the process of mapping out a curriculum that would be appropriate for those who would be pleased to "sit at my feet" as I opened God's Truth to their eager, hungry minds at the Academy. Near the completion of my quest, I observed the parchment with a good deal of satisfaction. In calling Maryam to my side, we shared its content together.

Here was a document that would set us on course to scan the basics of Christian theology and enable us to encourage a helpful balance between theory and practice.

CURRICULUM OF THEOLOGY

1
THE INSPIRATION OF SCRIPTURE
The Revelation of God
Guidelines:
/   \
Faith   Practice

2
GOD
Creator—Preserver—Governor

CROSS ROADS

Focus:
```
    /   I   \
Worship Witness Work
```

3
THE TRINITY
Theos—God   *Christos*—Christ   *Pneuma*—Spirit
Position:
```
   /     \
 Union  Equality
```

4
JESUS CHRIST
His Nature
Duality:
```
   /    \
Divine  Human
```

5
THE PRIMEVAL PARENTS
Created in innocence
Disobedience:
```
       /    \
Consequence  Sinful humanity
```

6
THE SAVIOUR
Yeshua—Jesus
Crucifixion
```
     /    \
Atonement  Salvation
```

7
THE RESURRECTION
Jesus, Alive! Ascended!

His role:
```
      /      \
Interaction  Intercession
```

8
SALVATION
How to be saved
Requirements:
```
      /     I     \
Repentance  Faith  Regeneration
```

9
JUSTIFICATION
Right with God
Believe—witness:
```
      /      \
   Grace    Faith
```

10
LIFE'S PILGRIMAGE
The Christian walk
Continuing on:
```
      /      \
 Obedience  Faithfulness
```

11
BLAMELESS LIVING
Hagios—Teleios
Holiness, Wholeness
```
      /      \
Be different, make a difference
```

12
ETERNITY
Immortality—Resurrection

CROSS ROADS

Judgement:
```
      /    \
```
Home: Heaven   Outer darkness

....

This curriculum is intended for *skole*, school, students who would come to the Academy following their general studies, on a selected day each week. My plan was, in the first year, to introduce the subjects listed—each month, a new subject. The second year would commence a more intensive study of each topic.

I would pursue the plan already proposed for the all-age group—I think we could name them the *Sunday Skolers*. We would meet for the class before worship and then share a meal together. Maryam suggested a brilliant scheme: while the more senior folk were involved with my class, she and other members of the leader team could take the younger children aside to hear, to act, to sketch the heritage stories.

The morning dawned on the opening of the new and, almost certainly, the first Christian Academy in the whole world. We tapped on Saul's door and found him fully ready for our walk to the address now firmly written on our mind and heart. We arrived early at the Meeting Hall so that sufficient tables and chairs would be in place for the arrival of our students—teenagers, married couples, elders—the preachers and the leaders—all ready to begin.

Barnabas began the morning's proceedings with a time of worship, prayer and praise. The new Headmaster was then introduced to his students. Something of my background was shared. A comment or two was made about my early years—those of "The Palace Peasant", the lad who grew up with King Herod Antipas! That I had been a student in the prodigious Rabbinic School at the Temple in Jerusalem provided sufficient foundation for my appointment as Headmaster of our Academy.

I must admit that this introduction heightened the expectancy flowing about the room. I rose and stood before the assembled Community of Faith.

'My friends—I think of you already as my friends rather than my students, for we are "family"! You have welcomed Maryam and me into the Community of Faith at Antioch and we shall be, as a family of God's people, sharing together—as *Christ*-ians— CHRISTIANS—the richness of the Hebrew Scripture.

This sharing of understanding will be paramount, rather than a thought of me as lecturer and you as listeners. You will find yourselves fully occupied in unravelling the mysteries that *YHVH Elohim* (The LORD) desires that you should know and cherish. We will open together the truths awaiting you.

'I promised your prophets and teachers—the elders in the Church—that I would commence our lessons with an ox, a house, and a camel.' Again, the shifting in the seats, the murmurings and mutterings. 'I will now disclose to you just how important are these three for they are part of a larger company comprising twenty-two in all. We will begin by naming their "stories" as "PICTURE PARABLES".'

I turned to the newly constructed chart board and, holding a piece of charcoal, began to write:

THE HEBREW ALPHABET
Picture Parables

'Let me explain. To understand the beginnings of the Christian Church, we must search the depths of its "seed-bed". Or, to put it another way: I now quote from the Scriptures revered by the Jewish people: *Look to the rock from which you were hewn.* (Isaiah 51:1).

'The very first of written words were merely scratches on a rock face! The people of God have been hewn from the truths of Scripture first found embedded in rock.' I turned again to the chart to illustrate my meaning and began to scrawl a series of scratches across the board which, none-the-less, made sense:

'At first, written Scripture was read, not as we do today! We must begin at the beginning—at the very first word in all of Scripture—but, to do this, here are a set of pictures!'

(We shall consider these pictures again later in the course)

'All, and I mean *all*, that follows finds its commencement as mere scratches upon a surface that would hold the message with a permanence not seen in the parchments of our day. Those scratches were not framed in words—be they Hebrew, Latin, or the Greek you know so well. The message that the scratches convey will be revealed.

'We must go even further back into the mists of great antiquity. The messages found upon the rocks in Egypt, Mesopotamia, Babylon or elsewhere, were not the messages framed in letters forming words! The messages of the most ancient times were framed in pictures, symbols, that held meaning in those long-gone ages of the past.

'My friends, we are about to delve into that ancient past in order to discover all the "Picture Parables" to be discovered in the Hebrew language—in both its ancient and modern format—so you may understand with greater comprehension its continuing power today to hold the truths of *YHVH Elohim*—the LORD God—the God of every clime and every culture.

'Now to relieve the mind of our elders seated here: the ox, the house, and the camel are the very first of the "Picture Parables" that open to view the wonderful riches hidden in the Hebrew language waiting for you to discover! Allow me to introduce you to this ancient art gallery. First then, to "A": the ox:

aleph

'You see before you now the first letter of the Hebrew alphabet. I have placed an **ox-head** into *aleph* (A) so you may see how the letter is framed according to the shape of the picture. The ox is the largest of all our tamed animals. It is the first, the pre-eminent: **the paramount beast.**

'In each letter of the Hebrew *aleph-beth*, that is, alphabet, the ancient scratching on the rock face may still be discerned by an astute eye. What may we learn from those ancient scratches? Friends: when we think of the word "paramount", what are other words that will emphasise the worth of the letter *aleph*?'

Answers came without delay: dominant, chief, foremost, predominant, first.

The Bible speaks today

'I promised that I would take you back to the very beginning of the Hebrew Scripture and to reveal how that which is ancient can speak powerfully to us today. Here we are at the very first, the foremost, the pre-eminent, verse of Genesis, chapter 1:

*In the very beginning, **Elohim** created the heavens and the earth.*

The Picture Parable

'I do need to point out that the first occasion where "the ox", the *aleph*, is written into Scripture, the sound is modified to indicate a soft 'e' to commence the Holy Name, *Elohim.* (Might I add a little humour here: it is assumed that the name given to the largest of all tameable animals on Earth, the *eleph*-ant, could have been modified similarly).

'On the first instance of its inclusion in Scripture, *aleph* stands at its most paramount. We will move into the 2nd chapter of Genesis to discover another important word commencing with *aleph.*

'Let it be seen that the human beings mentioned in chapter 1 were named as a species rather than by a given name. *Adam* is the name given to the creature—that is, *creat*-ion—for *adam* means, simply, "soil" or "red earth". The importance of "man" is not that both he and she represent the culmination of creation (man), but that ALL—both men and women—were made to live in harmony with God: to be like Him!

'What does the Picture Parable reveal about *aleph*—the ox?' The class began an animated discussion about the pre-eminence of *YHVH Elohim,* and of Adam and Eve—members of the paramount creation—who are equal in the sight of *YHVH Elohim* and should be so in our eyes.'

One of the elders emphasised the importance of some new concepts that the Faith Community were already receiving with grace from Saul of Tarsus: *There is neither Jew nor Greek, black nor white, rich nor poor, male nor female—we are ALL "one" in Christ Jesus!* (See Galatians 3:26-29). Wonderful, to hear such depth of truth to share with those so newly entering the Community of Faith! 'With each letter we will consider a related thought:'

A Point to Ponder:
'Who, or what is **A 1** in your frame of reference? **A**dd this: **A**stute **a**dults will **a**ctualise **a**n **a**chievable **a**im and are **a**lways **a**uthentic in **a**uthority.

'Friends, we have made a wonderful commencement. Now we

must proceed to the second letter: the "house". In ancient times, a tent was home. It framed the 2nd letter in the ancient Hebrew *aleph-beth*. Still today, the people of the desert rely on a tent.

Bedouin tent, *en route* to Beersheba

'But I'll sketch a house: the Hebrew letter *bayith* (we'll simplify the word to *beth*) is the 2nd letter. Added now is the most ancient form of *beth*, the Hebrew word for "**house**". Let us now observe the basic shape of *beth*:

Do you see how well the framework of the house fits into the Picture Parable? One can easily add the window and the door and there, is "home"!

The Bible speaks today

'You may be surprised to learn that the very first letter in the Bible is *beth*. By this letter the "door" is opened into the entire Scripture. The "door" is always open. It is always inviting. Genesis 1:1 states... Who can tell me what to write?' The words came as I proceeded to place the text on the chart for all to contemplate:

In the beginning, God created the heavens and the earth.

'Examples of the letter *beth* open up the door to *Bethel*. Please, tell me—if you understand Hebrew already, do not answer—what does the word *Bethel* mean?' Hands aplenty were raised. 'Please Sir, me Sir:' Yes, young lad, what is your name?' 'Basil, Sir'. 'Basil, please tell us what the name means.' 'Well, Sir, there's *beth*; that means *house*, Sir. And *El* represents the name of God. The word means *House of God*, Sir.' 'Well done, Basil!

'I'm so pleased to tell you that another town with a similar name is the town where I was born! It is a town that all will recognise who know the story of Jesus.' 'Is it *Bethlehem?*' 'Yes, indeed it is. There is the "house". The second part of the word is something that is baked over the coals each morning...' 'Is it bread, Sir? Is it bread?' 'Indeed, it is. *Beth-lehem* is *the House of Bread.*' The younger folk were fully involved now.

The Picture Parable

'I invite you each to come through the "doorway" of God's House to be nourished in the Word of Life. We may ask such questions as:
"When was the beginning?" "What was before the beginning?" and "Did God actually *create* the universe?"
Perhaps these, and other questions forming in your mind may come nearer to a resolution as we put on our spiritual walking shoes and go through the open door into new vistas that reveal God's omnipotent power. Right now, a further thought:

A Point to Ponder:

The "builder" who can bestow a "home" upon a house has believed the worth of binding the bricks with belief, behaviour, back-up and blessings that build the beautiful and beneficent.

'We come now to the final Picture Parable for today—the "camel":

gimel

'You may well ask what is the significance of a **camel** traversing over desert country. First, take heed of how well the picture of a camel is seen aligned to the form of the letter. Tell me, what are the qualities a camel?' I wrote up the responses: dependable, sturdy, reliable, tenacious, faithful, unfailing,

The Bible speaks today
'Genesis 1:16 states:
Elohim made two great lights: the greater light to govern the day and the lesser of the two to govern the night.

'In taking hold of the letter *gimel*, the ancient recorder begins to construct the word *gadal*, translated for us as "great". The **gimel** is certainly a suitable initial letter to be emphasising the daily trek of the sun across the sky. Though lesser in greatness, the moon has its drawing power, moving the tides to ebb and flow and granting the evening traveller a light upon the path. It also sets out the passage of the lunar month. It is enough to keep us on track.

The Picture Parable
'The path of the pilgrim requires the exertion of energy. Tell me, please—and now the elders, the prophets and the teachers, may contribute—what are the features of a camel that can teach us about trekking through each day as a Christian?' Their ready answers are worthy of recording in my journal:

* The path of a pilgrim requires the exertion of much energy
* It demands a sturdiness not only of gait but of character
* It needs endurance to conquer a daunting spiritual terrain.

A Point to Ponder:
'Our first session on the theme now concludes with this thought: The gait of the gimel (camel) is gainful as it grinds its way across the gravelled ground with grit and gumption. Its durability is indicative of the pilgrim who is guided by Godly goals with gallant grace.

'In preparation for our next meeting, please give consideration to the Hebrew word for father: *abba*. As I write the word on the board, you will notice that two Picture Parables emerge—both are doubled up—and you will now be able to recognise each of the two. The challenge is for you to share two qualities that may be found in fathers. One special thing to keep in mind: *abba* can be related to the term we use most often: dad.

'When next we meet, we will be walking through a "door", gazing through a "window" and hung up on a "hook"! The puzzlement returned though not the audible doubts. I became optimistic that our multi-aged class would consolidate into a viable Christian Academy! That many of the class stayed to engage in conversation with me was of great encouragement.

'Have you ever ridden a camel, Sir?' 'Have we made your home warm and comfortable?' 'Who is the "ox" in your life, Sir?' 'Could three pictures make one word, Sir?' It took some time to answer them!

3. A DERELICT VAGRANT

Saul was engaged in what appeared to be a serious discussion with Barnabas and Mark so Maryam and I made our way home. It was a bustling thoroughfare and we decided to find a shorter route. As it turned out, we came to acknowledge that it was a God-given route. In turning into a side alley, we came upon a poor wreck of a man huddled against a wall. We went to him.

Hardly allowing time to think, Maryam reached out her hand to him. The man cringed, shrank from her, turned his face from her. But something in her tender touch, her gentle voice then stirred a response in him that helped him look to her. Here was a man who lived with fear, emaciated for lack of food, hair and beard unkempt, clothes bedraggled and much in need of washing, mending—no, definitely discarding.

I knelt to him. 'Friend, you are needing a place to rest and something to eat. We would like to help you.' 'Manaen!' My beloved became quite animated. 'We have that extra room. There is a bed in it and there is enough food and to spare in the cupboard. Manaen, we must bring him home with us.' I saw the point and agreed with ease.

Thankfully, we detected no disease in this wretched outcast but it must have been some days since he had found a morsel to eat. We noted, as he staggered to his feet, that there was no great age upon him. In fact, I began to think that, maybe, he was yet a youth. A thorough cleansing and grooming would declare the wisdom of the thought.

Approaching our new home, we detected an apprehension mounting in his scraggly frame. I sought to ease his tension. And he listened. Those last few steps before we had reached our home became more purposeful. I think he realised that we meant him no harm. He straightened his shoulders as if steeling himself for what lay ahead.

I unlatched the door and held out a welcoming hand as Maryam aided his entry. He looked around in wonder and then turned his gaze on us. 'Why?' he muttered. 'What do you want from me?' Ignoring for the moment his question, I asked: 'What is your name?' The man paused, then muttered almost inaudibly: 'Onesimus.' 'Where is your home?' 'I have no home. I am just a

refugee.' 'What is your home country?' 'A land far west of here...
I will not, cannot return to it. I will live or die in Antioch.' With
that, he said no more until he repeated his question. 'What do
you want from me?' There was fear mingled with puzzlement in
his words.

'Onesimus, we demand nothing from you. We hold out our
hands to you. We welcome you. Would you permit me to bathe
you, to deal with the hair and beard? And, yes, you are of a
similar build to me. I have a new robe for you.' 'Why?' the
question came again. I thought to answer it in the best way I
could. 'Because we, too, are refugees!' My words would suffice
for the time being.

While Onesimus and I were engaged in the renewing of his
outer claddings of flesh and cloth, Maryam busied herself at the
fire, stoking, preparing the hobs for baking. With a certain
sadness, I observed the marks of slavery upon the lad, suddenly
surprisingly youthful. 'What do you want me to do with that
beard?' 'Take it away; get rid of it!'

With the many months of grime upon his body and hair
unruly and unkempt now gone, Onesimus surprised me with his
basically handsome frame. Our ablutions concluded, we entered
what we had named the living room. Maryam turned and her
face suddenly filled me with consternation. I thought she was
about to faint. Maryam uttered one word, 'David!'

'*Mimi*, dear-heart, this is Onesimus—our guest. Come, sit
down.' Maryam caught her breath, realising that the young man
she saw was not her son, slain by an assassin's wayward rock
during all the turmoil stemming from religious bigotry in
Jerusalem. As she gazed in wonder at the transformation in the
young man, she realised that David, the Jew, and Onesimus, the
Greek, were none-the-less of similar build and, more to the point,
similar in features and in stance. I looked again at Onesimus and
must confess that now I also saw a likeness so unexpected and
came to think that *Yeshua*—Jesus—was gifting us with a youth

who could take much of the grieving process from the heart of us. I endeavoured to explain the circumstance and it appeared to placate the young man!

With table set, Maryam and I sat in our usual chairs and made ready to eat. But Onesimus was not sitting down—he was beginning to satisfy his hunger over near the hobs. 'Onesimus, your place is here, with us.' His eyes spoke amazement, disbelief; his mouth failed to close! 'No, sir, I am a slave, I have no place that's equal to the master of the house.'

'Onesimus! Things are different in this home. Remember: we, too, are refugees. We have been made welcome here in Antioch. And you are welcome—as our friend. We have come to realise that there should be no difference between the servant and his master. We will regard you as "one" with us!'

In gazing at Onesimus, I saw tears welling in his eyes and coursing down his newly-shaven cheeks. I went to him, dried his eyes, and led him to his place at our table—servant equal with his host for the first time in his life, no doubt. Give him his due, the huddled heap crouching in the alleyway just an hour or so ago, was able to accept this dramatic change of circumstance with a grace which spoke well for him. As he picked up his fork and knife, hesitantly yet purposefully, I saw that here was a young man capable of accepting a new beginning to his life.

Late that afternoon, there was a knock at the door. Onesimus moved to the darkest corner of the room. (Soldiers? Come to arrest him?). The thought was written on his sensitive features. I opened the door to find Barnabas, Saul and Mark standing there with some degree of urgency. 'Do come in. sit yourselves by the fire.' 'We cannot stay for long. We came to you for it is imperative that you should know of your elevation to the leadership team of the Community of Faith in Antioch.'

'A leader? What do you mean? I do think that things went well at our inaugural session at the Academy this morning, but so soon, a leadership role?' 'Manaen, dear brother in the Faith, the Church is needing your expertise in leadership, now more than ever. We three have been assigned to carry the Christian message into new territory. We are to go westward with the Gospel! Oh, hello.'

Saul had seen Onesimus who had been trying to be as inconspicuous as possible. I introduced our "lodger". 'We met Onesimus on our way home today and have invited him to stay with us as other lodging was unavailable to him.'

Maryam spoke up. 'I have come to see that, if the Christian Church is to move on from its fragile beginnings, we must learn to balance our worship with our witness and our witnessing with our work. I have sensed a greater joy in my life since I became aware of the equal importance of the three: worship, witness and work. If we can manage all three, the Church will grow beyond these shores and go on until it reaches all the world!'

How I delighted in this new strength in Maryam to speak as she feels led. Perhaps it's been the recent emphasis upon the spoken word that there is no difference between Jew and Greek, rich or poor, male or female in Antioch! I was moved to put forward the suggestion that Maryam could also be a valued member of the leadership team. Our visitors saw the wisdom of the suggestion and promptly agreed with my proposal. And all the while, our house guest was taking in this remarkable conversation with undisguised amazement.

Onesimus was clearly interested in the conversation but I was aware that he had no understanding of the business in hand. Who were these men? What was their intention? What was the purpose for their journeying? It would take time to clarify so many things with him. For the time being, our goal was to help him settle into a place he can truly call his home and assure him of our continuing care and our hopes for him.

I wanted to know more of the mission to which the team had been called. Who were the people to whom they would go? What was the route? In answer to my questions, Barnabas then opened a piece of parchment on which was somewhat hastily sketched, I observed, a map that set out the direction of the endeavour. Together, we then scrutinised the route and realised that the journey would not be so difficult in terms of travelling. But these three men were about to set out on a new venture—the first of its kind. Together, they would sail into the most western region of Asia. The land journey would take them to another Antioch, the city of that name in Pisidia, and then on to Iconium, Lystra and Derbe before returning via a shorter sea route, to home.

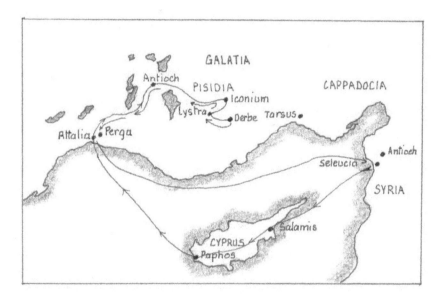

These three men were about to march into a territory which had not, as yet, so much as heard of Jesus, our resurrected Lord and Saviour. I realised that one of the people viewing the document at our table was also yet to be introduced to my *kebes* "Lamb", *the Lamb of God who would take away the sin of the world!* It would be the task of my beloved Maryam and I to make our Lord known to the run-away slave. Here was missionary territory at home, within our walls and windows! The worship, witness and work must also be effective on home ground.

Barnabas and Saul, with Mark taking on the role of their

assistant, were to set sail on the next high tide so it was time to bid them farewell. And so that they would fare well throughout this momentous journey, we took time to pray with them and to encourage them before they took their leave of us. 'Farewell, our brothers. God speed, good sailing, happy trekking. Through all the way, know that the Lord will take care of you. Abide in Peace: *shalom*.'

4. HANGING ON A HOOK

The second day at the Christian Academy began with bright sunlight filtering through the windows of home. The unmistakeable sound of a pot boiling on the hob had roused me from slumber. How come? A broad smile spread across my drowsy face. Onesimus! 'Wake up, Maryam, we are to be at the Academy before the sun goes down today! This morning, in fact.'

Breakfast completed, Onesimus waved us off. There would be no dabbling by us in his dishwater this morning. When we arrived at the now open doors of the Meeting Hall, we saw—to our great satisfaction—a larger group seated impatiently for the "door", the "window" and the "hook" to take shape. So, the three would reveal their secrets as the Picture Parables selected for today's lesson concerning our Christian Heritage were sketched on the chart for observation, contemplation and earnest consideration.

'Good morning friends. Before we begin today's session, let us pause for prayer as Barnabas, Saul and Mark have now set sail to commence the initial Christian missionary journey. They are carrying the Gospel further afield than ever before. Let us pray for their safety, their courage, and their effectiveness in conveying the Word of Life to the people of Western Asia. There were hearty "amens" and then we got down to the work prepared for the day.

'So then, to **Abba**: What have you to say of *abba*?' 'What about your *abba*, Sir?' I yielded to the quest and found myself utterly distracted for there was a benefit in speaking about Baruch of Bethlehem, who led his shepherd friends into that stable where the King born to be Man was found in swaddling clothes, with angels guiding them to that manger scene. And, of course, I did not fail to mention that I had been present in that stable when Jesus—the *kebes,* Lamb, was born!

I was not to be distracted for too long, however, for my *abbi* and the man also named *abba* yet—more truly—guardian: Joseph of Nazareth, led us to then consider what *aleph* and *beth* could reveal to us about fathers. 'Oh, *aleph* is the paramount letter, Sir. This must mean that *abba* is the principal person in the household. He is the most eminent of the family.' 'Does it mean the mother is of less importance than the father?' I asked.

The group mulled on that before acknowledging that both are of great importance but their roles are different. In fact, we take it for granted the mother acknowledges that father may be the final authority when it comes to family discipline. The father's role is vital for he is the predominant carer who must be prepared to give his life to save his "flock". There was general agreement.

'What of *beth*?' 'My father ensures that all is well within our home, Sir. In fact, Sir, he makes sure that we live in more than a house. We live in a home.' 'We can be secure in our home, Sir, because *abba* cares for us.' 'What of *YHVH Elohim*?' 'Are you saying that *YHVH* is our Father too, Sir?' 'Friends, the very first thing that Jesus taught his disciples about how to speak to his Father was this:

Our Abbi, who resides in Heaven, we hallow Your Almighty Name...
(*Abba*: Father, Dad; *Abbi*: my, our Father, Dad)

'What we have discussed this morning concerning the Picture Parables relating to *abba* apply as much to *YHVH Elohim*—even more so!' There was a murmur of approval. It was time to move into the "meat" of the morning. 'I present to you the fourth letter of the Hebrew alphabet (*daleth*) for it can teach us many things.'

The session continued on apace. 'What are the Picture Parables we may glean from **daleth**: "doorways", **heth**: "Windows", **vav**: "Hooks"? We enjoyed some hearty discussion. The third Picture Parable of the morning deserves comment:

.   (See illustrated alphabets—ancient, modern—located on pages 219–222).

vav

'What a magnificent picture is that of the letter known as the **vav**. How like a hook it is. Actually, that's exactly what it is! I need you to tell me the significance of this simple letter. Of what good is a hook?' 'Is it to hold ... to adhere ... to cling ... to join ... to grasp ... to grip ... to keep ... to make secure?' 'Yes! Yes! Yes!'

The Bible speaks today

'The **vav** holds two thoughts together, two phrases, two sentences, two actions, two entities together; **vav** is the conjunction: God speaks and it is done! At the beginning of time, time—as we know it—light "happens". This is the first recorded action of *YHVH Elohim*. The word "create" is not found here. The news is that God speaks and the action follows. Let me read the actual text. Note: the **vav** is the "and", the connection point where the two statements are held together.

*God said, 'Let there be light' and (**vav**), the light came into being.*

The Picture Parable

'In later Scripture (Exodus 26:32 and 37) the **vav** is to be found supporting the curtains hanging in the desert Tabernacle. The curtains were held in place by the hooks.

'In pursuing the thought of being "held", it is a profoundly beautiful thought to be held by God, to know the enfolding arms of the Almighty, the Sovereign, LORD. In the midst of deep sorrow or distress, His connection, His holding power is supreme. He will never let us fall. Let it never be that we would choose to sever our connection with God! Now, let's discover what can be said by way of:

A Point to Ponder

The **v**aliant who **v**alidate a **v**irtuous **v**iewpoint, upholding life's highest **v**alues, will **v**enture towards the ultimate **v**ictory AND their **v**alour will be **v**indicated.

'When next we meet we will be discussing a "seed", a "fence" and—wait for it—a "snake"! Shivers went up the student spines!

'Now, let me see, what will be your homework for the week? Please consider the Hebrew letter **vav**. When we meet again, we will think of the ways in which we gain assurance by realising that we are held by *YHVH Elohim.*

'And a challenge to the Elders who are fluent in the Hebrew language: think of the traditional Jewish greeting or farewell—one word, beginning with *shin.* What does that word tell us about *vav?*' I saw one or two smiles emerging on the features of the venerable gentlemen among us. I think the exercise will bless those men and everyone else when the secret is made known!

But now, it is time for home... How is Onesimus faring? Has he absconded? Will he come to feel truly settled in our home? As Maryam and I neared our new address, we shared our thoughts concerning Onesimus.

Here was a young man of great potential but he was new to personal hopes and desires. He had yet to look through the open window of possibilities. He had yet to unlock the door that had been closed so unfairly, it would seem, upon any potential yet to germinate in his soul.

Will he be waiting for our return or, has he taken his chance and moved on? The doubts remained with us until we opened the latch of our own front door. Look! Look! We'd had no time this morning to clean the breakfast dishes, no time to tidy our beds, no time to sweep and dust. Now, look at it: our home! Done and dusted! Truly so. The house was made to look like new and there was Onesimus with a smile which flowed almost from ear to ear. He knew that we were pleased.

I had to remonstrate. 'Onesimus, we do not expect nor require you to take on all the tasks of home. We three will share and share alike!'

'Manaen,' (he used my name! Joy! Oh joy), 'it is because you did not demand that I should take on the menial tasks of this home, that I was so very pleased to use my hands to please you both. By this, please know my gratitude for the kindness you have shown to me.'

There was a joy that was surely evident as Maryam and I sat with our new found friend to enjoy the meal he had prepared for us. Then, after he had gone to his own room, Maryam and I considered how best to record the blessings of the day. It was time for the writing kit!

The exuberance of the morning class had been multiplied by the impetus shown by Onesimus in, of his own volition, giving of himself in working through the day to please his hosts. Work is no drudgery if it is motivated by a desire to be useful, to be thankful. Yes! this must be the context of the poem which began to flow:

THANK YOU, LORD
(Choir: *Sardis*   8.7.8.7. Trochaic)

Thank You, Lord, for early mornings
When there's dew upon the lawn;
Here's the hint of Your own presence,
God is speaking in the dawn.

Thank You, Father, for Your blessings,
Flowing through us as we pray;
We will ever love and trust You,
Guide us to Eternal Day.

Thank You for the written Scripture
Where we find the words of life;
Lord, we claim Your precious promise,
By Your matchless grace we live!

Thank You, Lord, for friends and family,
Congregations that rejoice;
We will tell of grace and glory,
For salvation raise our voice.

Thank You, Lord, for care and comfort
When we falter on life's road,
For Your hand outstretched to help us,
As You share our daily load.

Thank You, Lord, for peace and pleasure,
Your companionship each day;
Thank You for Your timely counsel:
You grant wisdom for The Way!

....

5. PROFOUND PEACE

'Good morning, everyone. You have come prepared, I trust, to delve into the wonders evoked by those scratches on the rock face—the earliest form of sending messages. The Picture Parables contained in the most ancient form of the Hebrew *aleph-beth*, alphabet, reveal much of the heritage of the Faith we hold! Already, we have discovered how an "ox", a "house", a "camel" and a "door", a "window" and a "hook" can start us on our journey through all the written Scriptures.

'Perhaps the most important thing I can say as we commence today's discussions, is that the Christian way of discerning *YHVH Elohim*, cannot be fully realised until we are able to trace the Heritage of our Faith. Truth must be founded on Truth! We do know that the mission of Jesus is explained fully in the written Scripture. I heard *Yeshua*—Jesus—say one day:
I AM the Way, I AM the Truth, I AM the Life. No one is able to come to the Father except by Me. (John 14:6).

'My friends, Jesus is the only possible link with "The Father" for He and the Father are "ONE"! *YHVH Elohim* was not truly known as "Father" until Jesus came to Earth to make this astounding revelation: all who seek to know God through following Him who IS the Way, the Truth and the Life, are actually adopted into the Family of God. We are the children of God. We become heirs, together with Christ, of the inexhaustible riches made freely available to all who trust in Him. Rejoice in this Truth today!

'Our present challenge is to mine for the richest gems that are deeply embedded in the recorded Truth of what I will name here as "The First Testament". The day will come when a second, a *New Testament* must be constructed out of the experience of God's family. It is time for us to pick up our tools to do some investigating. We must prepare the ground for that Second Testament, for its content will be forged from what we are able to testify of Christ today!

'But I must not get ahead of myself. There was some home-work to be undertaken. How did you fare?' Ready responses were forthcoming concerning the **vav** and what its Picture Parable reveals about our wonderful relationship with our Lord Jesus Christ.

'You will recall that I asked the elders who are familiar with the Hebrew language to consider what the letter **vav** tells us from the traditional Jewish greeting that I now reveal as *shalom*. Simeon has agreed to explain the mystery!'

In taking the platform, Simeon—one of the major local preachers—began: 'Manaen, this has not been an easy exercise but what I have discovered—now that you are opening the Picture Parables to our gaze—is truly magnificent! I had to think a while about the place of **vav** in the greeting for its sound is never heard in the word.' Simeon took the charcoal.

'I won't steal our headmaster's "thunder claps" but this I will disclose: basically, we find just three letters in any Hebrew word though, occasionally, a fourth or more may be found. It is so with the greeting and I will now write it on the wall for you to observe the Hebrew letters required to vocalise the greeting that we know so well (though all is not quite right, as we shall see).

שלום

Shalom. No doubt you have already recognised the **vav.** Its placement is nothing short of wonderful. As I say, I will not speak

38

about the Picture Parables relating to the ש the ל and the ם though I will give the hint that there is something very special about that last letter—I leave it to Manaen to explain.'

'So, Christians—all—it is the **vav** which claims our attention. Something has happened to the **vav** in this wonderful greeting. It has become a vowel! In a language which does not really carry vowels, here is a vowel. Watch as I place a mark above the letter for **vav** to become "O". It is the extra letter and it is the glorious "extra" in the meaning of the greeting. Can anyone now tell me how **vav** can be the extra letter to complete the word?

A youth I now knew by the name of Alexander rose to speak: 'Simeon, I don't yet know what the Picture Parables of all the other letters mean but I do remember what the picture is for **vav**. (Sometimes pronounced **waw;** I prefer **vav**). The Jewish greeting is second to none for it tells us that *WE ARE HELD BY GOD!*'

Simeon, the African teacher, with a smile suffusing his shining face, bowed to me and then resumed his seat. I will certainly make use of the elder Simeon again in a future class. This insert to the morning's scheduled input has been of great value. 'Thank you, Simeon! This is a miracle that you have revealed to our fledgling Academy. *Shalom* to you!'

'We must own up! There is a spelling error on the board. All the Hebrew scholars will have noticed it immediately. It's the very last letter: the letter **mem**—the "raging sea". You'll see the sea! That letter is composed of waves ruffling up the surface of the sea. But **mem** has two Picture Parables! The raging sea is never to be found at the end of a word, much less that of *SHALOM*—PEACE. In the end, the sea is calm, at peace. And so is **mem**.' The error was erased to allow *SHALOM* to "tell" its true story: the extra letter in *shalom*—the "silent" **vav**—reveals that, because we are "held by God" our circumstance becomes calm!'

As the class was considering my discourse on the Picture Parable relating to the letter **teth**, we were confronted with the proverbial "snake-in-the-grass"! We pounced into a discussion on the disconcerting theme:

teth

'The serpent is detested by all. The snake is feared. Its entrance requires our swift exit. But do sit awhile! What are the words to place on our wall? Look! danger, opposition, confrontation, affliction, fear, antagonism, hostility, resistance, competition. Enough and to spare! See the picture fit the scene.'

The Bible speaks today

'Surprisingly, the Genesis text takes us straight to the light! *God said, "Let there be light" and there was light. He observed the light and saw that it was tov.*

'How very interesting! At the very first instance of its inclusion in the Scripture, **teth** appears as the initial letter of the word **tov**. The surprise is that, in the translation of **tov** we must use the word *good*! How can a fearful "snake" be in any way declared *good*?'

The Picture Parable

'What can possibly be the connection between **tov** and **teth**? You will agree that there is a "snake" lurking in **teth**. Quite so. But when the **teth** turned up in Eden, Eve knew no fear—nor did Adam, actually.

Why and how did *tov* turn to **teth**? 'The anomaly of such a situation must be this: goodness is only recognised in the eyes of humanity when the alternative—the evil—becomes obvious. We reach for the good when bad things happen. The sadness associated with this truth is that so often humanity has lost the way "home" to goodness.'

'Excuse me, Manaen, something comes to mind from what you are saying. Can I interject?' 'Most certainly, Simeon.' This revered elder then raised a matter of Scripture which was most pertinent to our stream of thought:

'There was a bronze serpent placed on a pole in the wilderness wanderings of the Israelites of olden days. That serpent was not meant to cause trouble in the midst of a pandemic where everyone was succumbing to a deadly disease. The serpent was meant to restore the health of the nation.'

'What a wonderful thought, Simeon. Thank you so much for reminding us of that dire situation. The antidote for the nation's wrongdoing was to look to the serpent on the pole. Of what other event in history does this recorded incident remind you today?' Hands shot up. I chose to ask Daphne, a studious young woman.

'It reminds me not so much of a serpent on a pole as it does our Saviour on that cross!' Applause broke out spontaneously. We shared the glory of an evil thing made *tov* from *teth* because of the One who allowed Himself to "become sin for us although He had never sinned" so that the souls of sinners could be made whole, good, *tov*.

'Now, as I draw this most illuminating session to its completion, I make this undeniable point: it has been ascertained that—with the coming of The Law, at first imprinted on two slabs of Horeb rock—the face of evil became more fully recognised. The Law points out the fault. It cannot rectify the affliction nor bring about the good (the *tov*). The Law of Moses (more correctly: that of *YHVH Elohim*) merely indicates the right path to follow. It took the sinless Son of God to rectify the scourge of sin. Evil can be very alluring; it needs to be recognised for what it is. Put simply, what is not good is bad! The good can be made manifest when the bad is acknowledged for what it is and a determination is made by us each to change our course of behaviour.'

As I was about to round up the proceedings, I became aware that someone new had entered the class. It was Onesimus! My inner joy was held until I presented:

A Point to Ponder
With the tenacity of trust, it is tenable to turn the tide where trials, tears, terrors and turmoil are transformed into tranquillity.

'Before you gather up your notes, I have a task for you in preparation for our next class: be ready to share some thoughts on how turmoil has been turned to tranquillity in your life. Now, who is a shepherd in our midst? Please stay awhile. I have a task for you.'

Maryam had already made contact with the young man who, so very quickly, was becoming integral to our daily life. Onesimus had entered the room as we were discussing the contrast between **tov** and **teth**. What had he grasped of the preferred **tov**? Had the discussion appeared *GOOD* to him? No doubt there would be time for some give and take on the subject.

Our return journey was in no way peppered by animated discussion. Onesimus appeared somewhat pensive. Perhaps he was taking time to allow all this new manner of thinking to seep into his conscious thoughts. All Christian concepts were quite alien to his way of thinking. It could not be otherwise for—as far as we could discern the condition of his past—it was impossible that any prior knowledge of Jesus had arrived on his home shore however far west that land could be. Only now Barnabas, Saul and Mark were carrying the first news of the Good News into the

western reaches of Asia. But, what of Greece? In time, perhaps...
No, certainly! I carry faith for that: Saul will see to it!

It would take time to share the Gospel—the Good News—
with a young man whose mind had yet to conceive that Christ,
the *Uios*—Son—of *Theos*—God—could in any way relate to his
circumstance. Yes, it would take time and, importantly, we
should not rush the lad. We must wait until the questions come.
In the meantime, may he see and hear from us the true
accounting of what it means to be a Christian.

'I have a surprise for you!' Onesimus suddenly became quite
animated as he opened the door to our home. He stood back to
allow us to enter and to discover that the table was already laid
in preparation for a repast that he promised would be ready
before the hour was done. The aroma of fish baking on the hobs
was soon evident. 'How come, young man? Fish for us today?'

'I've been known to catch a fish or two... Fact is, after you left
this morning, I hurried to the stream nearby and was so
fortunate to tickle the gills of this fish. Come, enjoy your fish!'

Meanwhile, Nicolas had resettled into his own environment.
It will be remembered that he had oversighted our escape from
Jerusalem after the death of David, our son. It was a catastrophic
period in our lives and the grief at times overwhelming Maryam
and myself was somewhat assuaged by this young man of the
"Serving Seven" in the Jerusalem Community of Faith.
Nicodemus had literally brought him to us on the day of our
escape as a young man of the Diaspora whose home was in
Antioch, of all places! Nicolas had promptly packed his bags, and
helped with ours, before we exited the city under cover of
darkness—close by the Palace of Herod Antipas but undetected,

thank God! Herod was not out searching for vagabond sisters at that time of night!

I was not surprised to find that Nicolas had gathered together six enthusiastic youths to rebuild the "Serving Seven", men empowered by the Holy Spirit to take control of the Church's ministry to the homeless of Antioch. Nicolas named his team "The Stephenos" in memory of his friend and colleague, Stephen, the first of the Christian martyrs. It must be said that "The Stephenos" were already providing a significant ministry.

It was of great importance to the whole Church that all the members of the Council were in regular contact with "The Stephanos" and adjacent services. As a member of the Council, I was able to keep abreast of the prophetic, teaching, and social services. That I was aware of specific needs could enhance the value of my teaching ministry. Bread in the soul is vital to the soul, bread in the hand is vital to the health of those we seek to serve. Lord, keep us well balanced in our daily ministry: in heart and hand.

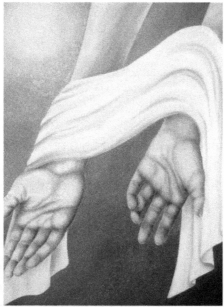

Painting "Serving Hands"

6.   A TEACHER'S TOOLS

Back in the classroom adjacent to the meeting hall, I returned to my theme:
'The human hand will play a large role in illustrating the great truths of Scripture via today's Picture Parables. However, before we get underway with what is new, let us reflect on the thoughts you have gathered concerning how turmoil has been turned to tranquillity in your life.'

One of the first to respond felt comfortable enough to disclose that there was still much turmoil in her experience. Homelife was anything but peaceful for her family failed to find a pleasure in her continued association with the Community of Faith.

It was imperative that all our students had opportunity to speak about their experience—particularly as it would relate to the journey through the shadows of grief's afflictions to the light of God's grace. As like reflections flowed around the room, I became aware of how vital it was that we should address the ever-recurring issues of grief and the ways in which it impacts on humanity.

I then addressed the group regarding the issue and I announced that—in the near future—we would commence a series of studies relating to how the Christian is able to cope with grief: that concerning the loss of loved ones, an inability to deal with the past and also the greater distress associated with what can be termed a continual, living grief—that is, the all-too frequent mourning because of a present trauma. 'Thank, you Manaen,' 'I will find that so helpful,' were among the responses of my students. I knew already just how I would frame the 2nd subject now confirmed in our curriculum. Time to move on:

I turned to our newly constructed chart board and began to sketch the Picture Parable that was first on my list for today: the **yad** (a hand), the **kaph** (the hand in action) and, the third for the morning: the **lamed** (the shepherd's staff). Because of the strategic nature of that staff, I will report on our class discussion relating to the Picture Parable selected for today:

lamed

'As I sketch the Picture Parable on **lamed**, you will all recognise the **shepherd's staff**. Before Alexander tells the story of his life with lambs, ewes and rams, we need to know the significance of the staff. Suggestions please.' I recorded the following aspects:
training, learning, discipline, education, guidance, coaching, teaching, instructing, correction, control.

The Bible speaks today

'Just five sentences in from the very beginning of Genesis, we are informed of how God was guiding, controlling, His creation:

God called the light 'day' and the darkness He called 'night'. There was both evening and morning [as a result of His work].

'The preparatory phases of creation are astounding. Following the first creative act by which the heavens and the earth came into being, God had now prepared surfaces on which the light was able to shine. Again, the Scripture does not state that God created light. He allowed light to shine.

'We have two men in our company today whose names mean *light*. Can anyone name these fortunate people?' There were no raised hands. The class was turning this way and that to catch a clue. At last, I named the duo: 'Lucius and Lucas, please stand. Tell us something of the light of God that has found a place to shine in your soul.' We were blessed by the responsive testimonies.

The Picture Parable

'Alexander is going to present for us his daily use of the shepherd's staff now revealed to you as the *lamed*—the 12th letter in the Hebrew *aleph-beth*:'

Alexander warmed to his task. It was the life he knew and loved. There had been no prompting from me as to what he should or should not say though I knew as much as most about the pleasures and the perils of shepherding: my father, Baruch, had been a shepherd all those years ago out on the Boaz Hills of Bethlehem.

It was as though we were out there, tending his sheep with Alexander, caring for his lambs, guarding and guiding the ewes and rams. Many of our key words of the morning were re-emphasised through his discourse. A hearty round of applause greeted his eventual return to his seat among the class. We finished with:

A Point to Ponder

Learning without leaning toward a legitimate lifestyle is like a river without levees—it lacks discipline and the logic to liaise with the laudable and lead another to the Light.

Bernice then came forward with her harp and, while she made ready, I explained that the singing of a hymn could bring another dimension of blessing to a lesson that leads us naturally into worship.

It was simply a must to introduce the Shepherd's Psalm—written by the shepherd boy who had been chosen by God to guard and guide his people as Israel's King: David. Maryam became quite emotional as she had recited the Psalm that was so much part of our own Christian experience. Following Maryam's rendition of the Psalm, I continued:

'Friends, I have written a poem, the words of which you now see attached to the chart board. It relates the story of the Good Shepherd—the Shepherd who is the *Pastor* of our lives! Bernice will introduce you to the tune she has composed so that we may sing together King David's Psalm of the Good Shepherd (Ps. 23):

THE SHEPHERD'S SONG
(Choir: *Amazing Grace, Crimond* C.M.)

My Shepherd is the Lord of life,
He calls me to His side;
His pastureland is all I need
For He's my faithful Guide.

Refreshment comes from sparkling streams
Where purest waters flow;
My Shepherd's path is righteousness,
His Name is precious now.

Sometimes in shadowed trails I tread,
Through valleys of deep grief;
My Shepherd's there and comforts me;
He grants my soul relief.

Each day I'm fed from His own hand!
When evil threatens me,
The Lord draws near to cleanse my wounds;
Mine is the cup of joy!

His goodness never-failing, sure,
His kindness when I roam;
These blessings sanctify my days:
My Shepherd leads me Home!

The ensuing discussion was of great value as we considered

48

the staff and the rod carried by a shepherd whenever with his sheep. Why? I gave emphasis to the fact that the staff is for the benefit of the sheep, the rod is to deter predators. We considered the ways in which "The Good Shepherd" leads us each day out from, and back to the fold. What of the fields, the mountains, the valleys, the wilderness?

The students were invited to give description to their daily lives—their experiences as a "sheep" in our Shepherd's care. The class was quite stimulated and I gave extended time to the exercise for I perceived that it was feeding their souls! 'Keep in mind that the crook on the staff can pull the sheep back from disaster. In that sense, the staff is a guide, an aid to discipline, a teaching tool!'

'My final word for all this morning is that the *lamed* has two roles to play when at work with the shepherd: it is meant to be assisting him in **guiding** and **guarding** the flock. Allow yourselves the discipline—the *disciple*-ing—of the Good Shepherd. He is our Guide and our Guard. Follow him in the paths of righteousness.' I was to discover, before the week was through, how very important that advice was to a couple who had quietly taken that advice to heart.

Undetected, Onesimus had slipped into the classroom and was now seated, listening, though I saw no movement of his lips to join in singing the recently composed hymn. Perhaps our new friend had never found opportunity to sing, had never found anything worth singing about. He came home happily enough with us.

After our shared meal was completed, Onesimus began to fidget. 'Manaen, I heard some strange things this morning. I have observed the lot of a shepherd from a distance in my former life. That man told his story very well. I did understand where he was coming from. I liked that word *pastor*. You said that it was a word well suited to the leaders of the Community of Faith—whatever that means.

'Manaen, I've thought about the word. I think it describes you very well. You have become like a "shepherd" to me. I would like to call you Pastor Pa—I rather like the Latin "Pater". Would you object to this?' 'Onesimus, my dear young friend, if what you caught from this morning's class encourages you to look upon me as your pastor and your "dad", I could not be more pleased, more moved, more encouraged. Here we are, refugees together. But we have found a refuge and yes, I will be your pastor and, yes, I will care for you as a father would!

I thought of *abbi*, Baruch, the shepherd whose son had now become also a shepherd—a pastor pa—at least in the eyes of one who knew nothing of Christian principles and practice: a Greek runaway slave, "adopted" into our family. Onesimus! Is this young man beginning to accept new concepts of life and living?

But Onesimus had not finished his requests. 'Oh Maryam, I begin to look upon you as the mother I never knew. May I call you "Mother M?" Mouths at first agape and then allowing uncontrolled, but joyous laughter to escape, we shocked the lad. 'What is wrong? What have I said? Have I upset you?'

'Onesimus,' I explained with undiminished joy, 'it's your accent. The "M" sounded just like *emi*. You have all but spoken the Hebrew word for "*my mother*". It sounded just fine to us! Do you see how well the initial "M" has fitted into your request?' 'Then, may I call you "Mother Mother"... Well, perhaps Mother *Emi*?' Maryam was bereft of words but the tearful hug she gave to her new charge told him all he needed to know. We were *family*.

7. PERMANENT PROMISES

The Academy appeared to be gathering strength, both numerically and in terms of ready responses and eagerness to learn new truths. The group was never afraid to interject with a timely comment, question or observation that enhanced the content of the theme.

We were now more than half-way though this initial course. It had been planned specifically to reveal the deeper reaches of the heritage out of which the Christian Church—first known as such at Antioch—emerged. The Picture Parables proved to be a practical way of turning the keys and opening doorways into Truth which strengthened our grasp on the purposes and the imperatives of the Faith we hold.

It was difficult to gain any information regarding the progress of Barnabas, Saul and Mark. Were they still alive? The journey would be hazardous. The listening capacity of a people steeped in the religions and culture of their regions would not be conducive to a ready acceptance of such revolutionary concepts of belief. We prayed for them. Daily!

A hand-delivered letter came unexpectedly and, when the seal was opened on the missive, much of our fear was assuaged. As we read John Mark's report, it was realised that their many problems did not outweigh the progress made thus far. The mission team was about to move on to Antioch in Pisidia and would then set their sights on Iconium, Lystra and Derbe.

As brief as this initial written report was, we discovered that the sea voyage to Cyprus was uneventful. The Gospel was preached in the Jewish synagogues at Salamis and then in Paphos. I had to admit that most of the locations listed were quite new to me.

Although some spitefulness had broken out at the hands of a vindictive sorcerer, the proconsul—a man by the name of Sergius Paulus, reputed to be an intelligent man—was not deflected in his search for Truth. Saul was now known as Paul and, though this new name emphasised the diminutive build of the man, he stood like a giant in putting the sorcerer to shame.

The proconsul had been so impressed by the message that he believed the words of the missionaries and came to faith in Christ! We hoped that a further letter could be sent as the men went further into untried territory. It was doubtful for now the trek would be by foot over long miles of questionable terrain. I must keep that report. The thought was forming in my soul that all Christian records must be filed.

I had warned the class that the next Picture Parables would find them tossed about in mountainous "seas", and they would be needing to "swim upstream". But, never-you-mind! An adequate "support" will be found.

The various responses to my hints at the coming themes by now had led into undisguised inquisitiveness. I was happy to have the group moving out from classes with some expectation of what might eventuate when coming together next Sunday for the study of Scripture in the hour before worship in the Community.

During the week that followed, two visitors appeared at our door. Maryam was closest so answered the knock without delay. A young man named Eustace and, at his side, a beautiful young woman whose name still escaped me, stood before us. 'Good morning, to you Maryam and Manaen. Angela and I decided to come to you to seek advice.'

'Come in, come in!' Seating was arranged and Onesimus took his leave of us. Some grape juice and crisp biscuits were made available. The minutes needed to clear the plates and cups of our brief repast allowed our visitors to relax.

'Manaen, we need your help, and Maryam's too. We are promised to each other—we wear the *arrhabon*, engagement, ring—and the date for our marriage is just a month or so away. The thing is, since we have become part of the Community of Faith, we have no desire to make our vows before the idol of *Aphrodite*. That block of stone can give no guidance such as we desire, ah... require. We want our marriage to commence in the presence of *YHVH Elohim* with our friends.

'Manaen, it is one thing to make a promise to someone who is greatly loved but we will need guiding and guarding—those are the words I have already gained from your teaching and we intend to put them into practice. Is there a way that we could make our marriage vows before the assembled Church?'

I saw the commencement of something very precious here. The Christian Church could become the centre where all those desiring to be truly committed to a marriage could find it possible to make their vows in the presence of the LORD and together with our spiritual family in the Community of Faith.

'What is the nature of the promises you desire to make to one another in God's viewing?' 'Our promises will be the same. What I vow to Angela, Angela will vow to me.' I noted a vigorous nodding of her head—in the affirmative! 'Allow me to open up my writing kit. I would like to make some notes of what you do intend to say to each other and to all assembled on the day.' Parchment and writing tools at the ready, I asked for their comments. Both contributed to the discussion. They had obviously planned it to be so. As their comments flowed, I rejoiced in their mutual love and their determination to place their promising into the hands of the Lord.

'Our marriage will last until our dying day!' 'It will last through joy or through pain.' 'It will remain whether we become rich or stay poor.' 'Whether we are sick or well.' 'Our aim is to love and to cherish each other all the days of our life.' 'We will live to please one another in the continuing sight of God.' We will declare these promises most solemnly and emphatically. We will stand undeterred by anything or anyone!'

I found it most difficult to keep up with them. The statements, uttered convincingly, were quite remarkable. If promises such as these can be kept by both the groom and bride, the LORD will surely bless their union. This fact was acknowledged and I offered then to pray with the young man and his beloved of the *arrhabon.*

'We will make plans accordingly and, when the leadership team have had an opportunity to consider the proposal, we ask you both to come to us again so that the final preparations can be made.' We shared a happy time together of discussing their backgrounds and ours so that we could appreciate more fully the testimonies of faith that were forthcoming from each.

When next our class met for *SCRATCHES ON THE ROCK FACE*—the series on the most ancient form of Hebrew—the students were ready for some surprises. The letter **nun** (which, appropriately enough, follows **mem**: the raging or calm "sea"), allowed us to focus on a unique moment in the process of the creation of the universe! It does call for some recording of the happenings of our deliberations that morning.

Nun

'We will be staying with the waters but now, we will find ourselves in the water, swimming—if possible—upstream! You are a "fish". What are the abilities that will allow you to swim against the current?' Endurance, continuance, fortitude, persistence, strength, resolution, hope were written on the chart.

The Bible speaks today
'Genesis 1:20–21 brings us to the fifth day of creation. There is a strategic movement in God's program to create all that the eye can see—throughout the visual universe:

God said, 'Let the waters bring forth the creatures that possess the gift of life.' Therefore, He created all marine, then flying creatures.

'On this, the fifth day, a unique word: **bara** has been used for the second time. It will be used on just three occasions. It occurs in the very first verse of Scripture: *In the beginning God created—**bara**—the universe*—the heavens and the earth. And now, as late as the fifth day, **bara** is found for just the second time. On the fifth day, God brought *LIFE* into being: creatures have been created!

'Let us take a pause. I have been speaking of the "days" of creation. I'll test your memories: what do you recall from our previous studies about the meaning of the word "day"?' 'Manaen, you have reminded us that this word can convey more than one meaning.' 'For example?' '24 hours, sir.' 'A period of time, sir?' 'An age?' 'Could it mean an "eon" of time, Sir?' 'It will depend on how we use the word. Most times, it will mean a day comprised of 24 hours. It must be remembered that the first chapter of Genesis is a Hebrew poem. Those who choose to write in this way are prone, at times, to utilise what is known as "poet's licence". There are those who maintain the writer recorded a 24 hour time period. Others are not so sure.

'Many who "profess" a *skolerly* approach, maintain that a far greater time-frame is required. They put forward the feasible point that it took a great expanse of time for the dry land to appear out of the "deep"; it takes time for grass to grow in order to become the food for animals—a later creation. But to the fish now.'

The Picture Parable

'Fish are remarkable creatures. There are species that are able to swim in depths that would crush a sunken vessel. Fish were given fins: the capacity is theirs to swim upstream, against all currents of adversity. God created all creatures to be "at home" in their environment—including humankind. What are the "fins" of humankind?' 'The fins of faith, sir!' 'Class, hold that thought! It is vital to our present studies. We must set about determining just what it is that makes humankind so very different from all else that preceded us.

'Genesis 1:24–27 reminds us that the **materials** were already at hand. Then, **movement** had been generated within living creatures. What yet needed to be achieved for the creation of **man**? The soil was made ready: the first creation. Life had been gifted to otherwise inanimate objects: the second creation. What made humankind: the third creation—*bara* is used just three times in the Genesis records—different from the sea creatures and land animals already in existence?

'The third instance where *bara* is imprinted on the Genesis record is the crowning glory of all creation. Living creatures already possessed the gift of life. What more was needed to complete God's creative activity? We are created to be part of God's family! We are created to **know** Him and to realise that we know Him, to **live** in accord with the principles He has set for us, and we are given the capacity to **enjoy** Him forever! Humankind has the ability to **commune** with our Maker!

'We know who we are. We know, and we *know* that we know. This is knowledge that exists beside the knowledge that is held by the mind. The knowledge that exists together with our mental faculties is SOUL knowledge. It has a special name. Surprisingly, the word is given to us by the Romans—Latin, to be precise.' Audible groans aplenty peppered the air. 'Actually, the word must be seen in two parts.' Interest flared again. 'CON: *with, beside* joined to SCIENCE.

The students in our group are, of course, aware of science. The class began to see the point of the introduction of this word: the soul holds the knowledge that stands beside knowledge. 'We possess both head knowledge and heart knowledge, Pastor.' The leap from "Sir" to "Pastor" did not go unheard!

'It's time that humankind acknowledged their "inner voice". Class, what does conscience do for you?' Ambrose rose to testify: 'My conscience informs me of when I am doing right and when I am doing wrong. It also informs me of the consequences of each.' 'Yes, indeed!'

'In looking again at the chart, what is the word that stands out for you? 'Hope'. 'Hope'. 'Hope, Pastor.' 'This is a word that must not pass us by. Living in hope that you would include this wonderful word in your description of the Picture Parable relating to *nun*, I have asked Maryam to read my poem on the theme.'

HOPE

The past is history,
the present is our task;
the future is our hope
of all that's yet to be.

Undreamed of possibilities, amazing powers
of intellect, adaptability, prowess beyond
immediate sense lies just beyond the hills
of current circumstance. They beckon us!
The skills with which inventions manifest
allows us scope to raise the edifice
of our accomplishments will be surpassed.
Possessions, pleasures, grandiose amenities
beyond our present ken lie out of reach
the while, but they will come to us—
our human ingenuity will see to that!
And, in the midst of them, our hearts
will ache. The barrenness of superficial aims
will send us to the depths of human poverty
and dread beyond all countenance will test
the mettle of our character unless, in us,
there is a growth of goodness, grace, and
gentleness such as may now embrace
this fragile world.

The past is gone,
the present nearly done;
the future holds our hope—
it's in the hands of God!

A Point to Ponder:
The naming of humanity, last in the creative process, as the first of all creatures is notable for it is in our nature to be numinous. We hold a new-found hope and now we should never negate God's Voice.

'Are we left to sink or swim all by ourselves? Not at all! Our studies have reminded us of the **vav**—we are "held by God".

....

58

8. THE SEVEN SENSES OF LOVE

The intervening days had given me an opportunity to take hold of Saul's (oh yes, Paul's) conversation with me concerning three great words so expressive of the Christian's lifestyle: FAITH, HOPE and LOVE. My writing kit was called into service once more. I prepared, hopefully, what could be a fitting introduction to a grand announcement to the Church at Antioch. A poem was inscribed on my waiting parchment:

FAITH, HOPE, LOVE, THESE THREE

*FAITH goes on, into the mist
of all that's yet unknown, with hand
outstretched to One who comes, unseen,
but truly known. Heart warmed, assured,
it matters not what will or won't betide,
the hand is firmly held. That is enough!*

*HOPE looks ever up, into the azure sky
of aspirations yet unfolding, always bold.
Trusting arms upraised, there's confidence
in One who comes to lead through all
the upward, onward way of life, in touch
with His Eternity. Such is Hope's proof.*

*LOVE reaches deep within, to where
the heart plays out its rhythms of the soul.
The harmony of kindred lives, held close
within the grace of God, prepares the way
for One who comes to forge a blessed unity
where Faith, and Hope, are drawn from Love.*

Therefore, the greatest of these three is Love!

'Friends, there is no better place for me to *announce* that there is an announcement to make! I call upon Eustace to come forward. It is only right that he should make the news known.'

Somewhat shyly Eustace stood, then made his way slowly to where he would be in view of all. 'You will be aware that Angela and I wear an *arrhabon* ring. We are promised to each other. Please come, Angela, stand by my side. Together, we now share our news. We will be married on the first day of next month...' Loud applause—both verbal and by hand—interrupted his speech. Now Eustace had gathered confidence. 'We have requested that Pastor Manaen conduct a service newly framed, for Angela and I desire that our vows are made in the presence of the Lord. *Aphrodite* has no place in our promises or our marriage! We invite you all to join the celebration. We shall pray together and then feast together: one and all!' All decorum departed for a time and no one cared about the lapse in the lesson of the day.

At last, order was restored but not before a bridge was built between the news and the Picture Parables. I saw that, really, these were linked! 'Friends, as you are only too well aware, my speech continues to be flavoured by the language of my youth. Because the Greek language is the *lingua franca* of our times, I am able also to converse with you in your "mother tongue". I trust there are not too many false spellings or pronunciations in what you must hear from me!' Gentle humour filled the room. I find these people are so kind.

'Three great words have been introduced to me by Saul—now Paul—I trust he will provide a discourse on the three one day. In his absence, allow me to utilise the three: Faith, Hope and Love. Let me see if I am able to express your way of articulating each. Our chart will help us here:

FAITH	*pistis*	crunches doubt to gain confidence
HOPE	*elpis*	quenches despair to gain confirmation
LOVE	*agape*	crushes dislike to gain Christlikeness'

'Pastor Manaen, *confidence*—the word you have chosen for what it is we gain through faith—means just that very thing! You have reminded us of the value of the first syllable—*con*. It means *with* and the second part of the word is drawn from the Latin word for faith—*fides*!' 'Linus, a good point, well taken. Just think of it. Every time a doubt is crunched under the foot of faith, our confidence is strengthened.

'What of Hope?' 'Well, Sir, for some fun, Sir: '*elp is* ours for despair is pushed out of the way through Christ. He IS our Hope!' 'Yes, Dorion, good fun, though not only fun and fancy: you have made a most *help*ful statement. Certainly, Christ IS our Help, our Hope!'

'My friends, Maryam and I are mindful that, in your language there are four magnificent words used generally to place LOVE in its correct "basket". Indeed, there are more. We will discuss the seven major words which relate most specifically to LOVE. I think we may need more than one chart attached to the board this morning!

THE SEVEN SENSES OF LOVE

Storge 'The unconditional love known between a parent and child.'
Melancton spoke up. 'How do you know of this Pastor? You have no children.' A gasp was heard. I knew from whence it came. 'I am at fault. I should have informed this Community, which really is our family now, that our only son, David, was killed by an assassin's stone. It is the reason why we now live in Antioch.' To ease the shock of the lad, I said, 'Thank you, Melancton, you have given me the opportunity to share our story with you. We know the strength of *storge*.

Philantia 'The love of self.' I then put on an act. "Oh, look at me!

How well I dress today." And that's enough of that. Let's get on with the list.

Ludus 'The love known as "flirting". Now, now. Eyes to the front. No giggling please!

Pragma 'The love that keeps on keeping on! *Pragma* is known by friends, lovers, of long standing who respect, care, honour, and cherish each other.

Eros 'The love that describes the romantic, passionate forms of affection. Eustace and Angela can tell you much of this and also, every married couple in this room, I trust.

Philia 'The love that is known and shared by good friends. Often this delightful experience is also shared by the others listed.

Agape 'How could there be a seventh Love? There is no room for yet another love in this swelling heart of mine, you declare? What is there yet to bear in terms of love?'

A thoughtful silence allowed, from me, a further comment by which to rouse a response or two: 'Who is yet to be represented on this list?' Some answers were forthcoming then. I quietly disposed of them by pointing to another item on the list. It seemed no inspiration loomed. From whence could I draw a positive suggestion regarding *agape* love?

Ianthe offered this gem: 'Pastor, could it be the people that nobody likes?' I could have kissed the lass! Instead, I danced upon the spot. 'Yes! Yes! Yes! This is the unlikely love, for an unlikely people! This is the love that Jesus requests of us. **Agape** love is that which the Christian feels for the less fortunate, for strangers, those in need of comfort and of care and those who do not expect to find any kind response.

'Oh! Look at the time. perhaps we should close down for today and pick up the threads next time we meet.' 'Pick them up now, Pastor, pick them up now.' I heard the repetition of 'Yes', 'Yes', 'Yes'! So, we settled in to discover how the Picture Parables could in any way relate to the Seven Senses of Love.

We had arrived at the letter **tsadhe**. What would my cherished class contribute to this wonderful Picture Parable? The modern form of the letter was attached to the chart I had prepared for the day. Soon, the class were involved in sharing their thoughts on what the sketch conveyed by way of a parable so that their input could be added to the chart.

tsadhe

'You see before you now, the letter **tsadhe**. What should I sketch to provide a Picture Parable? 'That's easy, Sir. It's a mother with her child. It is **storge** love.' 'As the mother nurtures her child?' 'Yes Pastor! It's assistance, nearness, help, love; to bear, nurture, sustain, hold, cooperate, benefit.'

The Bible speaks today
'Genesis 1:26–27 allows this wonderful insight into the plans of *YHVH El Shaddai*: *God created humankind in His own* **tselem** *[image, likeness].* Then there is an immediate repetition to confirm the event:

So God created [bara] humankind in His own image, in the image of God, humankind was created; male and female He created them.

'It's all very remarkable!' 'How so?' 'Two key words, Pastor Manaen: the word **bara**: used on only three occasions, here—on the third—it is used three times. That's emphasising the point. And then, **tselem**—with the initial **tsadhe**—is also used three times. The LORD really wants us to get the message!' 'And,' Dorion interjected, '*And Elohim said...* I've never noticed it before. Pastor, why is the title of our ONE God written in the plural?'

'Excellent question, Dorion. From the very beginning God's Name has been written in the plural. Genesis 1:1 proves the point. How can ONE be more than One? "Trinity" is undeniably discerned throughout Scripture—God: the Father, God: the Son, and God: the Holy Spirit. The Scriptures reveal that the THREE are ONE: undivided in essence and co-equal in power and glory.'

The Picture Parable

'Friends, what does the text say?' 'It declares that we are created in the image, the likeness of God but how can this be so?' 'Pastor, Pastor, Pastor.' 'Yes, Melancton?' 'We, too, are "triune beings"!' 'How so?' 'Sir, we possess a body that is not the mind and we possess a mind that is not the soul!' 'Yes, Melancton, body, mind, and soul: that we are and yet we can differentiate between the three. What is more, I don't carry someone else's mind, and another's soul in my body. I am "one".

'We are fearfully and wonderfully made! For God to be a Triune Being, it must be that three Divine Aspects of Love are actualised: One who loves, One who is loved, and the Love itself: Father, Son and Holy Spirit. Here is **tsadhe** in its most profound form: the Christian is nurtured, held, discipled, disciplined—in the very best sense of the word—by our loving Father, God: *Elohim*—the *im* turning the word into the plural form.

'Jesus taught us to pray by using that beloved word: *Our Father, Abba, who resides in Heaven, Your Name is honoured and adored. May Your will be done on Earth in the same way it is done in Heaven. Father, grant us today our daily bread; please forgive us when we do wrong; lead us not into temptation's lures and keep us from evil. We know it is Your Kingdom to which we belong, we are held by Your power and all glory is Yours. Amen.* (Matthew 5:5-15)

'Pastor, if we are truly made in the image of God, no wonder He loves us and gave His Son to carry to destruction all the sin and the sins we should have borne ourselves. That is the best care any parent can give to a child. It is **tsadhe** love Manaen.' 'Thank you, Simeon. You say it well for us. Together, we have found the third link: the link of LOVE. And I will stress, God's love is **agape** Love—the greatest of the three: FAITH, HOPE and LOVE: together, they form a powerful guide for Christian life.

We will complete today's study now with:

A Point to Ponder
The **ts**addikim [righteous guides] will employ wisdom in leading their students through their trials and tribulations. **Ts**unamis, overwhelming tides, will ebb and flow: be equipped for high tide!'

The students were somewhat mellowed by the flow of our discussions but there was a discernible warmth in their conversational murmurings during the break for refreshments before worship commenced.

9. "THE BELLS ARE RINGING"

The dawn spoke well for the day. The calendar had no need to inform us of the date. It was the first of the month. This was the day when Eustace and Angela were to be married.

Our wardrobe was certainly not bulging—due to our refugee status—but Maryam and I were able to don our garments with a pleasure upon us. 'Would you like to join in with the celebrations,

Onesimus?' 'I think I would. I've never attended a marriage in my life and I would really like to see a ceremony where *Aphrodite* will not be asked to bless the bride and groom. Yes, I think that I would like to come with you!'

Folk were filling the room. Seats were difficult to find. Onesimus had decided on a seat at the back. He was an observer, not a participant. Maryam found her place beside Bernice, the harpist—they had a special role to play today. Flowers enhanced the beauty of the room. Two candelabra and a central cross had been placed on an ornately carved table that had become an altar before which I stood in readiness for the entry, first, of Eustace who marched confidently down the central aisle. He stood by me, then turned to watch, in awe now, of the beauty of his bride glowing in her flowing gown of glistening white. The harp provided music that enticed an acknowledgement that what was about to begin would be most memorable. This music aided Angela's approach.

The bride and groom turned to face each other, ready to make the promises they had prepared during the evenings when they met for counsel together with Maryam and the marriage celebrant: me!

We began with prayer. The Lord had brought this couple together, their months of the "earnest", the *arrhabon*, (the guarantees they had given in their promises) were enhanced by their keen desire to walk in accordance with the will of God. Prayer is not new to them.

'Friends: we have gathered together on this, the first day of the month, to celebrate the marriage of our good friends, Eustace and Angela. Both have requested a new way in which to make their marriage vows. In this holy place, we have come to witness their dual dedication and their solemn declaration that nothing stands in the path of their future happiness which would cause a stumbling block.' Both the bride and groom smiled at me, then uttered their assent.

'Eustace, do you declare before all gathered here that you intend to hold to the promises you make this day?' 'I do declare it now.' And, Angela, what is your response? 'I will love, honour, and respect Eustace all the days of my life.'

'Eustace, now speak your promises before the Community of Faith.'

'I speak to all assembled here.
These are the promises I make today:

Angela: I take you now to be my wife.
I acknowledge that you are the love of my life.
Our marriage will endure: through the best or worst of times,
whether we become rich or remain poor,
whether our health is good or weak.
I will love and cherish you always, Angela.
I speak these words before our Pastor, our friends and
our Lord!'

'Angela, what is your response?'

The people, listening to the promises, heard those same words again, repeated joyfully. It was clearly seen that the promises were made, not only from the lips, they flowed spontaneously from the heart.
I spoke again to Eustace. 'You may now place the wedding ring upon the finger of the one to whom you've spoken all the promises.'

'In the presence of your family and friends and before God, may He bless this marriage! I have the privilege to announce to all that, from this time, you are now man and wife together. This is a marriage sanctified before our Lord Jesus Christ. Now may we all provide our promises that we will seek to guide, to guard, to assist, support this couple, known and loved by us all.

'Before the Benediction is pronounced, I have requested that a hymn of blessing be sung. The words are a paraphrase of Saul's early teaching in this place, though I don't know if he has recorded this as yet. The prophets and teachers in our midst have instructed me. Maryam, who has a fine contralto voice, has learned the words and—with Bernice—has composed a melody whereby the poem becomes a Psalm:

O LORD OF LOVE
(Soloist: *St Margaret* 8.8.8.8.6.)

O Lord of Love, today we pray
Your blessing give, so rich and free,
As friends have come their vows to pay
And, in their love, to ask that You
Will guide through all their way.

Lord, You have taught us love is kind,
Patient, enduring, suffering long.
No evil thought ensnares the mind
When love does keep no score of wrong;
Your love as one will bind.

True love holds fast, will never fail,
It bears all things, its hope is sure.
Though knowledge won't always avail—
We know in part—we do know that
True love will never fail.

We see today through clouded glass,
But, one day, face to Face with You;
While life shall last, You'll bless our days.
There now abides Faith, Hope and Love:
Love stands all tests, always!

Now, set Your seal, Lord, on this love,
As these before Your presence bow.
Lord, You once came Your love to prove

And called us to abide in You—
Abide with us in Love.

'Friends: in this, the Church at Antioch, the first Christian marriage service has been conducted. May it stand at the forefront of all such marriages that are to come. The format of the ceremony will change but not, we pray, the sentiments expressed in this new way so that the vows made before the LORD will only gather strength as the years go by.

'I commend Eustace and Angela to you now. Please, join with me in the Benediction that I draw from our heritage:

May the LORD bless you and keep you,
May the LORD make His Face to shine upon you,
May the LORD shower His grace upon you,
May the LORD lift up His countenance upon you
And grant you His shalom peace.
Amen.' (See Numbers 6:24–26).

It was a joy to sit at table and to feast in celebration of the marriage and to see how well the bride and groom mingled with the assembled crowd. They are truly at home with us all.

The day took a new turn upon arrival at our home for, barely had we sat down to recuperate from all the festivities, Onesimus began to comment on, and question, many aspects of the marriage ceremony.

'Pastor Manaen, this morning's marriage has challenged me in many ways. First, and foremost, I guess, is my wondering if ever I will find a person to whom I could or would make such promises. The thing I find most difficult to understand though is how on Earth can you direct your prayers to someone you cannot see. As much as I refrain from bowing to carved statues such as the goddess *Aphrodite*, is it not better by far to recognise a god that is seen to exist?

'Onesimus, what is a soul?' 'I've never seen a soul; I cannot tell of it.' 'Then, let me see, can you describe the human mind?' 'That's easy Manaen. It is the place where the brain stores all the unforgettable things it's learned.' 'What does it look like?' 'I don't know. I've never seen the... Oh, there are some things that exist which cannot be seen?!' 'Exactly. It is the same with the human soul. The body is not the mind. The mind is not the soul. Yet, if you set your mind to it, you will discover that, deeper—more profound—than the mind, there is a human faculty that gives direction to the mind so that the body may activate what's good and decline the evil inclinations which occur from time to time. The soul advises the mind, the mind informs the brain to activate right principles and practices.'

'Pastor, that's beyond my capacity to comprehend today. I will have to think about that. I suppose I will need to react to what my mind tells me. But, "soul"? I can't come to terms with that right now. Let's change the subject. Who is Saul—the man you sometimes refer to as Paul?'

It was time for Onesimus to hear something of my experiences at the Rabbinic School attached to the Temple in Jerusalem. It was so good to be able to describe the man once labelled—by me—the "Terror from Tarsus". Maryam joined in with her account of how we met Saul again. 'We disembarked from the ship by which we had barely escaped with our lives after David's death, to land on the shores of Syria. Saul met us at the ship to escort us to Antioch. He had been transformed. He is now a new man because he met with our Lord Jesus Christ.' 'I would like to meet that man one day.' 'Perhaps you will. But for now, let's rest awhile.' Onesimus relaxed.

10. THE CRUX OF EVERYTHING

The tapping on our door was brisk and I hurried to discover who would be calling so late in the afternoon. There was Lucius and another who... Surely not! Impossible! Incredible! 'John bar Zebedee! You "son of the thunder-claps"! Come in, come in. Maryam, look who has arrived with Lucius to visit us!'

The usual rounds of 'How are you?' 'Keeping well?' 'How long is it since we last met?' completed, we settled down with some light eats and a thirst-quenching beverage to engage in some serious conversation. John had come to investigate the Community of Faith at Antioch. The work being done here, John explained, would greatly assist him in his aim to build the Church in fields afar.

'Where will you be heading, John?' 'I have already journeyed far into areas of Asia, where the news of my beloved Rabbi Jesus had never been heard. I plan to bring together people who are willing to receive the *Gospel*—Good News—that there is One God and it is Jesus who reveals the Truth.

I plan to emphasise that *God so loved the world that He offered up His only Son so that all who will receive this Truth may be saved from their sin.* (John 3:16). Even if it takes a lifetime, I will not be deterred. You see, I am a fisherman who has been called to "fish" for humanity and, if I need to sail the oceans of the world or merely march the ancient cobble-stoned paths of Earth, I will not be deterred!'

'Where do you plan to set up the churches of which you speak?' 'I plan to return first to Ephesus—I've already met some quality people there. Then, northward to Smyrna—the people of that city are poverty stricken and they suffer much hardship. Friends, I'm discovering that the word we know for witnessing is out of date! These days, *martyrdom* can demand much more than being prepared to speak up for the Lord. In some places, like Smyrna, to speak up for Jesus is likely to take a man to his death! I have stood appalled at the harsh treatment meted out to Jesus' followers there. Pergamum is scheduled as the follow on.

'Next, I will move on to Thyatira—I've already found some

believers there who are willing to serve and be faithful to the Lord. Sardis will be challenging—the people in this city have a great reputation but many find it hard to live up to what they profess. I have found that the Philadelphians are really *philia-delphians*—good people, friendly and supportive of the stranger in their midst. And I must include the great city of Laodicea—I'm loath to describe what I have found there for, superficially, all seems superb: the citizens are wealthy, industrious and healthy. But they have no inkling of their pathetic plight. My work will be difficult to maintain in Laodicea. How will such people recognise their true condition?'

'You must take some time to recuperate after your gruelling trekking these many months. But may I request a special task for you?' Lucius said. 'As you are aware, the coming Jewish Festival of Passover is set down for this coming Friday. We have given a new importance to the Festival for we will utilise the season to emphasise the suffering, death and resurrection of Jesus. *Easter* from now will mean the "New Spring".

'Manaen will commence the Friday morning worship service by bringing to a completion his "Initial" series—I say that advisedly—on the Picture Parables abounding in the Hebrew language. He has provided the Community with a fascinating art gallery though what the final picture is, I cannot begin to imagine however much I've tried. I've yet to see the point of it. Manaen promises to surprise us though and maintains that it is in keeping with the theme of the day.'

Lucius had not determined, obviously, the nature of the final Picture Parable! John, I noted, looked at me with a conspiratorial smile. He was aware of what that final illustration would convey.

'Johanan, John, could you present the main message of the Friday worship service? It would be wonderful to hear the Gospel from the heart of one who stood by our Saviour on Mount Calvary.' 'It will be my joy both to share with you in worship and to testify to the amazing event where the Jewish Passover has been transformed. We can now celebrate the greater Passover: the sinner need not die! The LORD forgives, Death "passes over" the repentant sinner. Jesus' ultimate sacrifice made our salvation certain! Oh, I'll have plenty to say!'

I interjected then. 'John, would you be able to find some time between now and Friday when we could discuss a plan that is forming in my mind which may be of great value to all Christians everywhere—those of today and down through the future too.' 'You intrigue me, Manaen. I will always have time for you anyway! Two days from now. Reasonably early in the morning but allow me a "sleep-in" if there needs to be a reason for my late arrival.'

The intervening day found me engaged in furious debate with myself! I needed to prepare for the unveiling of my final Picture Parable on what could be thought of as "God's Friday". But the plan that had been germinating in my mind for some considerable time: what would John think of it, would he give some assistance to the scheme, how would he find the time for an on-going commitment that I saw most plausible but, would he? By the time John knocked on my door, my plans were clarified but my nerves were still on edge. I did not want to land further burdens into the hands of this committed warrior.

'So then, Manaen, what is this great plan of yours?' 'You certainly jump right into the briny, so to speak, John! Let's see: where should I begin? As you know, I have been engaged in the Community of Faith—the Church at Antioch—to open up to new eyes the Heritage of The Faith we hold. I chose to take our students right back to the very beginnings of recorded Scripture. The Hebrew *aleph-beth* has assisted me to explain complex issues like the creation of the universe in terms more readily acceptable to Gentile minds. The series has stimulated debate, pertinent insights and the ability to stay the course.

'Midway through the series, a letter arrived from Saul of Tarsus—we know him now as Paul. He's been transformed. I had sometimes think that he's been re-made!' I used to call him the "Terror from Tarsus". He is no longer terrifying but always forthright: the strength of his argument is seasoned with grace!

'Well, the point of it all is this: I've been engaged in opening up the written Scriptures—The Law, the Wisdom, the Prophets—for we realise that the Gospel cannot be fully understood without acknowledging the "soil" from which it sprang. The need for a sacrifice to pay the purchase price for redemption is realised by an acknowledgement that the crucifixion of our Lord is God's gifting to humankind. It is our responsibility to bring that Truth to light.

'To get to the point, that letter to which I referred included some truly magnificent accounts of people on the Island of Cyprus, who have received Christ as Saviour and Lord of their lives. I have placed that parchment in a special file and this is what I want to suggest:

'I now see the written Scripture as our heritage. It must never be forgotten or cast aside. It is the First Testament but it is now, to my mind, the *Old* Testament. John, we are in need of a Second Testament, a *New* Testament!' I saw a light in the "disciple–apostle" eyes. But then the question came.

'This, indeed, must be achieved. But how do we begin?' 'John, I can advise, I can gather, I can collate, but I cannot write the Gospel Truth. I need a man like you, John. Yes! You. Is it possible that you could find some time, somewhere, to write your record before its potency is lost?' 'But, Manaen, I've already begun! I've actually brought my first manuscript to share with you today. I have not forgotten your expertise in The Law and the Prophets while at the Rabbinic School in Jerusalem. Nicodemus had informed us of the mark you made upon that school. Will we ever see the like of Nicodemus again?

'So! May I share the beginnings of my Gospel with you now?' A vigorous nod of my head was all John needed to unroll the parchment gripped firmly in his hand. John began to read:

THE PROLOGUE

'At the beginning of time as we know it, the *Logos* already existed.
The *Logos* was with God for the *Logos* was—and is—God.
It was through the *Logos* that all things were created.
Without the *Logos* was not one thing made that has been made.
Life dwelt in the *Logos* and that Life was the Light of humankind.
This Light continues to shine in the darkness
and the darkness has never been able to extinguish it.
A man named John came to bear witness to the true Light
so that, through that Light, all people may believe.
John, the Baptiser, was not the Light. He came
to bear witness to the True Light that enlightens
everyone: the *Logos* was coming into the world.
The True Light was in the world—the world that had
been made by Him—but the world failed to recognise Him.
Yet, to all who received Him and believed on His Name,
He gave the right to become children of God, born of God.
The *Logos* became human and made His home among us.
We have seen His glory—the glory of the *Logos* who came
from the Father to gift us with grace outpoured on grace.
From the fulness of His grace, we receive blessing upon blessing.
The Law came via Moses, but grace and truth came through
Jesus Christ—the *Logos*—THE WORD: "The Articulation of Divinity".

I all but leapt about with joy! Never had I heard a statement expressed in any form that could equal this profound commentary of the Person we know as Jesus Christ, the Anointed, the *Messiah*, the Saviour of the world, now recognised as The Eternal Son of God: the "Articulation of Divinity".

'John, you must continue. The world must hear, must read, must tell the Gospel: The Good News! Will you find the time and energy to place on record what you've observed when *Yeshua*-Jesus opened to your view the mysteries of Heaven? I will endeavour to support you in any way possible. John: I am available!' 'Manaen, I have already mapped out the structure of my Gospel records. Would you like to see them now? I have not much to show for my thoughts but, it's a starting place.'

'Oh, please, let me see what you have done. I would keep in safety here at Antioch any work you wish to keep secure. I believe that now we have the beginnings, the building blocks, for the construction of the "NEW TESTAMENT".' Together, we scanned the parchment notes that one day would be recorded comprehensively and known as St John's Gospel. The building up of the New Testament had begun for here was the outline laid out on the table before my dampened eyes.

'There will be a strong thread of the story that will weave each segment into a seamless whole but I have chosen to structure the account from the major columns that are "built" on the foundation of the Prologue. The lists provide the basic outline of this Good News. You will discover that I have a strong inclination to build on the number 7!

EVENTS

1 Feeding of Five thousand :
2 Healing of man born blind :
3 Directive: one entry to Life :
4 Debate: Wayward leaders :
5 Raising of Lazarus :
6 Finding, knowing, receiving:
7 Branch connected to Vine :

CLAIMS

1 I AM the Bread of Life
2 I AM the Light of the world
3 I AM the Gate of the sheep
4 I AM the Good Shepherd
5 I AM the Resurrection, the Life
6 I AM the Way, the Truth, the Life
7 I AM the True Vine

DISCOURSES

1 The New Birth
2 The Water of Life
3 The Divine Son
4 The Bread of Life
5 The Life-giving Spirit
6 The Light of the World
7 The Good Shepherd

ACTIONS

1 Cleansing the Temple
2 Miracles becoming Signs
3 Preaching and Teaching Ministry
4 Confronting religious leaders
5 Triumphal entry to Jerusalem
6 Crucifixion
7 Resurrection

THE HOLY SPIRIT

1 The 'Paraclete'

THE SEVEN SIGNS

1 Water Changed to Wine

SACRIFICE

'Manaen, watch this space!' With those hearty words, John began to roll up his parchment to await the filling in of stories, discourses, miracles, tragedies and triumphs that would enrich the parchment already waiting for the chapter that would follow on from what was to become The Prologue.

John knew where the story would commence. I would have to wait. But then, I think I know that John, in memory's path, would be hurrying down to the Jordan River for this is where the Messiah was identified by "The Baptiser" as *the Lamb of God who would rid the world of sin*!

'Oh, before I take my leave of you, Manaen, it will be of great interest to you that I have had some recent conversations with Matthew—you will remember the erstwhile tax collector—well, he has already begun to bring together his thoughts on some parchment, too. He explained that his plan was to focus on the Kingdom of God. Our Rabbi often used the kingdom model as a meaningful description of what the Kingdom of God may be like. He has chosen to utilise parabolic teaching in order to emphasise the nature of the Lord's message. I'm sure that will find a very pleasant place within your thoughts, Manaen—the resident "parable provider". I can tell you of his current address.' He promptly wrote it down.

As I farewelled him from our home, I asked John if he would mind me writing a new Psalm that would express the thinking in his Prologue.

There was no hesitation. 'I hope you can have it ready for our worship period on Friday for, if it doesn't fit in there, my Prologue also will need to be reshaped.' 'Manaen, allow your Psalm to speak of the One we have come to know—in this Gentile "world"—as the *Logos*. Let the *WORD* be proclaimed in power on "Passion Day" and every day: in your Academy and on my "rocky road" as I begin to build the Seven Churches.

'Manaen, a prayer: "Lord, give us strength for the tasks You've placed in our heart and hands. Bless us, and make us a blessing as we focus on Your death and resurrection on Passion Friday that the Church may grow in strength and influence. Amen." *Shalom*. I'll see you soon!'

John's departure sent me to my writing kit. His awesome description of the beginnings of time and space reverberated in my mind. Could I capture something of its majestic grandeur that will open eventually into John's recorded Gospel? Today it was my privilege to endeavour to embed the wonder of his words— surely inspired of the LORD—into my waiting soul:

CREATOR GOD
(Choir: Tune: *Ode to Joy, Europe* 8.7.8.7. D)

Word of God in the beginning,
Called the formless void to light;
Voice of God commanding order
In the chaos of the night.
Dawn has come in golden glory,

CROSS ROADS

Christ has formed the universe;
He began creation's story:
Spoken is the Mind of God.

Son of God, the Lord Eternal,
Once was clothed in human clay;
Co-existent with the Father,
He displays life's brightest ray.
Light that shone on Earth's first morning
Has revealed hope for the world;
Christ has brought us faith's new dawning:
Open is the heart of God.

Light of God, forever shining,
Through the gloom of sin's dark night,
Glowing with the joy of Heaven,
Shining on the human plight.
Radiant splendour, not declining,
Light that night can't overcome,
All our human life refining,
Token of the grace of God!

Power of God with life abundant
Moved to heal the human blight;
Mighty Word of God declaring
Evil's curse has had its night!
He's the Light now intervening,
Giving all to set us free;
All our bonds have lost their meaning,
Broken by the Love of God!

....

It was time to prepare for "God's Friday" and for the concluding Picture Parable within my "Initial" series—as Lucius had declared it so to be with his humour giving emphasis to the dual aspects of the title. Fitting. We have been engaged, throughout this initial term with the "initial" letters of the Hebrew *aleph-beth.* What would my class make of the most ancient sign representing the letter **tav**? (This letter may also be read as **taw.** I prefer the "**v**"). How will the dramatic nature of the sketch that must stand with that final letter be received by my class, so sincere, so inquiring, so ready to believe?

The meeting hall was well prepared for this was to be a very special day. After our usual, informal greetings, I commenced our proceedings with an acknowledgement. 'Good morning, class. The Academy reaches the conclusion of the first course in which we have explored together our Heritage of Faith and, in doing so, we have been observing the written records of the creation of the universe. What a very good place to start!

'I confess before you all that there is no evidence of the most ancient form of the Hebrew language having been formed by an amalgamation of Picture Parables that add nuances of meaning to the message being conveyed. But it is my hope that you have found the series to be spiritually stimulating and beneficial in terms of hearing more profoundly than is normally the case, what the inspired word of God is saying to us today!

'Certainly, there is some value in pursuing the viewpoints indicated in the Picture Parables. As you become more familiar with the Hebrew language you may find that this process will open up a deeper understanding of God's word for humankind. For our final session, see now:

tav

'Our first view today is that of the modern letter **tav** or **taw**. What could be the illustration most suited to add to the letter facing us?' 'It's a peculiar shape, Pastor.' 'It's nothing like a full stop, Sir.' 'It's really not like anything, Sir.' 'It doesn't have a good base, Pastor.' 'Is it weak?' 'That is for us to determine!'

The Bible speaks today

'What is the last word to be said about this remarkable *aleph-beth*? Genesis 1:1 carries a word of just two letters, usually found adjacent to *Elohim*—God. The word is את, (*at*). Most often the word remains untranslated. It's just there! What can be so strategic as א and ת you ask?' Joy! Oh joy! John leapt to his feet. 'Manaen! Here we have the One who is the "First" and the "Last"! This is—I will utilise the Greek alphabet: "*The Alpha and Omega*"! This Name is found in the beginning of God's word? I promise you now, I will strive to make sure that it is in the very last chapter of the New Testament that is yet to be written: the record of the One who is, truly, "The First and the Last"'. 'Who is this visitor?' was written on the surprised features of most present. I would bide my time with the introductions for the major disclosure of the entire course had yet to be imprinted on the mind and heart of my class.

The Picture Parable

'It is time for the last word! Come with me to the writings of a major prophet of the Jewish people. Ten Clans had been crushed by Assyria. Those that remained had been dragged as captives into Babylon. There they remained in exile for about seventy years. Yes, a lifetime. The prophet, Ezekiel by name, sought continually to bring comfort and counsel to the captives. Ezekiel was in daily communication with *YHVH*, the LORD. Ezekiel was a praying man. At times, he was overwhelmed as he became involved in powerful visions.

'It is in the ninth chapter of his great prophecy that—at last we discover the most ancient form of the letter *tav*. Let me explain.' 'Add the "scratch" sketch, Pastor.' 'What does it look like, Sir?' 'Wait awhile. We must get to the *why* before the *what* today for this is the Passion Day!' 'Yes! Yes! Yes!' came from the stranger—John—in our midst.

'Ezekiel tells of being "hauled" from Babylon to Jerusalem in a vision and overhears the LORD instructing a scribe—you are aware that I was once a scribe in Jerusalem but, mark you, I'm not as old as Ezekiel—God needed a scribe to undertake this amazing mission:

Go throughout Jerusalem and place a **mark** *on the foreheads of all those who grieve for the city's circumstance.* (Ezekiel 9:4).

'When that sentence is translated into Latin or Greek, the word **mark** is inserted for, to Gentile minds, it makes most sense. The point is interesting but hardly earth-shattering. What is the greater clarity provided by the original Hebrew? Instead of **mark**, the word is actually **tav**. What, then, is the illustration that brings us to the last Picture Parable?

'In the most ancient form of Hebrew, surely utilised in the 6th Century before the coming of Christ, before the marching of Roman feet across our sacred land to raise the hated crucifix, the mark—the sign—that would reveal true righteousness, the shape of the letter ת was very, very different. And it is all we need to know to place a final exclamation mark upon all our studies thus far.

'Friends: I give to you the sign written on the foreheads of the faithful, the righteous people as witnessed by Ezekiel.' I took the charcoal and drew a † upon the **tav**. A stunned silence held all in shock. I paused so that the class could absorb what had been disclosed. When we returned to a reasonable state of normality, we were able to rejoice in the power of the cross!

'Before the last full stop on "the last word", I must draw your attention to the FIRST WORD! Yes, friends! I will now take you back as far into recorded history as one can journey. The first word contains …

the most astounding statement in the history of the world!

We will observe those first *"SCRATCHES ON THE ROCK FACE"* to catch the wonder of it all. And you are now capable of reading that word and discovering its amazing message.' I heard some "oohs" and "aahs". 'Watch closely now:

בראשית

'What is the first word in recorded Scripture?' 'If that's the first word, Pastor Manaen, it must read as more than one word.' 'Correct. And what does the word say?' '*In the beginning*, Sir!' 'Indeed, it does say that. But we will now attempt to recall the Picture Parables. On the first morning of this series titled: *"SCRATCHES ON THE ROCK FACE"*, I presented a word in the most ancient form of Hebrew and promised that I would reveal its meaning. I now bring you into the "tent"!

Reading from the right: what is the first?' 'That is the "house", Sir. It reads as "in."' 'Very good. What is the next? Yes, Neoma?'

'That one is easy, Sir. It is the "head"'. 'Thank you. I will put the two together: we will discover another word. We will build up the message that the word reveals via the chart':

בַּר *bar*   **This is the Hebrew word for**   SON
         The first message in all Scripture!
         The "HEAD" (the "SON"), is in the "HOME"

א *aleph*   **The most Prominent Person of all:**   GOD
         We have discovered GOD as FATHER!
         *(A)Elohim is **abba**!*

ש *shin*   **Here is the TOOTH that grinds, crushes: CRUSHED**
Teeth have the power to kill!
Do we discover here a SON who DIES?

י *yod*   **We discover the HAND that kills:**   **GIVEN**
GOD loves the world that much!
He was prepared to give His Best: for US!

ת *tav*   **The Picture Parable—the MEANS:**   **CROSS**
We now view again the most ancient form
of the first word in recorded Scripture:

'In greatest antiquity the CROSS was raised:
Jesus IS *The Lamb (THE SON) slain from*
the beginning of the world.'

Before I could continue, the visitor—John bar Zebedee—stood up. I saw that tears were welling in his eyes. 'I've known the word *b'rashith* since my youth. I've never seen it so! Manaen, the whole message of Scripture is revealed in that one, that first, word! Manaen, let me speak the truth held in that first word found at the beginning, in Genesis 1:1.

God loved this world so much that He gifted His only Son so that,
through Jesus' crucifixion, the "whosoever" need not perish:
They may have ETERNAL LIFE! (John 3:16).

Nothing more needed to be said among this gaping congregation of people who would also wear the sign of a CROSS if need there was so to do! Perhaps a time could arrive when the Roman armies will demand of this people a renunciation of the Faith they hold for here is a people committed to The Christ of the Cross-bound Way! Consider, therefore:

A Point to Ponder
Those who remain true to their testimony, trusting in the Lord, will triumph over all the trials and tragedies of transgression.

> * (See Appendix—pages 218-222—for the complete Hebrew alphabet, ancient and modern, with related data to observe each of the related Picture Parables).

'As we draw this extensive study to its conclusion today, I have asked Maryam to lead the entire company gathered in this meeting hall in a new Psalm that has emerged from my writing kit. You have become familiar with the melody Bernice has selected. I've placed the words upon this chart so let us worship in song before I introduce our visiting preacher.' The room was now buzzing with anticipation. Who was the mystery guest to whom all eyes had turned?

CALVARY
(Choir: *St Margaret* 8.8.8.8.6.)

Christ's cross was borne to Calvary,
The Lord of life was called to die!
He counselled those along the way
Who wept for Him in grief that day:
The King born to be Man.

Christ's cross was raised on Calvary,
A scaffold for the world to see;
He came to set the prisoner free
And gave His life for you and me—
Redeemer, Friend and Guide.

THE CRUX OF EVERYTHING

Christ's cross was meant for Calvary,
For there a thief put in His plea
And found the Kingdom's shining ray:
In Paradise that day he'd see
The Saviour of the world.

Christ's cross enhances Calvary,
For it became a place where we
May come to seek His pardon free
And live so we'll forever stay
With our Eternal Lord.

Christ's cross stands at our Calvary,
He said, 'Come, now take up your cross,
And follow Me today. This cross
Is meant for life, not death. Today's
Call is: now live for Me!

'I now present John bar Zebedee. John is the leader of today's worship service.' Already voices were raised, injecting a keen sense of anticipation. But when I added: 'John was called to be a disciple of Jesus and, following our Lord's resurrection, I am able to present him as the Apostle John!' Thunderous applause all but made the roof fall in.

John came to take my place and proceeded to set the scene: 'I am John. With deep emotion on this special day, I am able to inform you that I stood near the cross on the day that Jesus was crucified.

'I saw Manaen also stand near the cross at Golgotha—*the place of the skull*—and he heard what I will convey to you. Manaen, what do you most remember?' 'As I watched the Man I knew to be the *Messiah* die—taking the burden of our sins upon Himself—I came to faith! When I saw no hope for Him, I heard Him say, '*It is finished!*' I realised that His words were not those of despair but of triumph!

It was when I had seen no hope for Him, the scales fell from my eyes. It was His Mission—as *the Lamb of God to be the sacrifice who would save the world from its sin*—that had been completed: finished! Jesus has made it possible, for ALL who are willing to trust Him for their ultimate salvation, to enter into Eternal Life!' 'Indeed, Manaen. That's what I heard but I had to wait until Sunday—the third day—before I realised the truth of it.'

John then continued with his treatise: 'My aim for our worship meditations today centres on **Shadows** and the *LIGHT*. What turns night to day? How is it possible to walk out of spiritual darkness into the Dawn that shines into our lives, leading us into the Light of Eternal Life?' It is only possible through the Light diffused by the One who is *THE LIGHT OF THE WORLD*. All who follow him shall not walk in darkness but have the Light of Life!'

John then emphasised his treatise with an illustration:

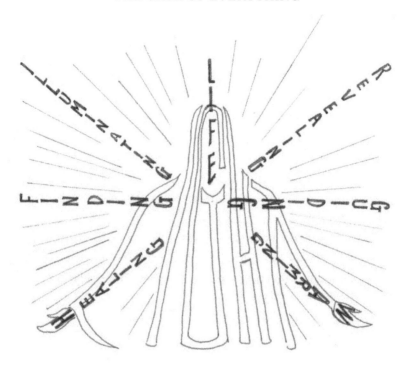

In his closing stages, John brought that exultant Community into a deeper understanding of the Faith they hold central to their own being by using the words of his Prologue—in particular, the words which had such resonance with the great event we now celebrate:

> *To all who receive Jesus as Saviour, He gives the right*
> *to become children of God, born of God...*
> *He has gifted us with grace outpoured on grace.*
> *Jesus came to tell us what God is like—He came to*
> *ARTICULATE GOD'S LOVE: HE IS "THE WORD"!*

The dear man concluded his address by reading my paraphrased rendition of his wonderful Prologue. I was deeply grateful. The morning concluded with many extemporary prayers: spontaneous, heart-felt, as the company rejoiced. Then, as John packed away his parchment, he beckoned me.

'Manaen, I have been giving further thought to our project. If we are to ensure a comprehensive coverage of the Gospel News, we must look for the right man to tabulate the miracles—particularly those of the healings. A medical man would be best. No one comes to mind right now but be on the alert. We may need to tell of many happenings of which he would not be aware.

Oh, and keep your eye out for a younger man than us to encapsulate the action stories of our Lord—the Man we have sometimes referred to as "The Nazarene". I must be on my way. Pray for me, Manaen. We will meet again to share what could be labelled "the building blocks of the New Testament".

I hugged the man! By this plan, including Matthew's intent, we would have four accounts of the Gospel: The Good News! Once one catches a glimpse of the vision the Lord implants in the mind, its form takes shape. Foundations laid, pillars raised and the finished product comes to mind!

Detail of larger painting "The Faith We Hold"

11. THE SCENES OF SORROW

'Maryam, we need a break! It's more than time we walked the streets of Antioch to gain a better understanding of our new environment.' The weather was warming considerably so we strolled at leisure—a very pleasant pastime—and sat a while to speak with citizens and the many visitors who thronged the streets of this great city. Antioch had made us feel at home in this new, Gentile world. There was much that warmed our hearts even as the sun began once more to warm our bones and relentlessly maturing bodies!

The academic term had ended and a follow-up would soon be "knocking at the door". The major subject for the second course of study had already been selected. It had emerged from the reaction of our class to a painful topic and the resultant discussions had confirmed our intention to present a series on grief and how a Christian is able to deal with sorrow, mental distress and the suffering of the soul.

Because of the nature of this course, I had asked Maryam to take on the major aspects of this most sensitive of subjects. My *Mimi* princess had encountered, experienced, much that fitted the theme. I had promised to support her and contribute where I could be of value as we proceeded with our plans. It was time to speak of the personal implications implicit in this course.

One evening, after all the cooking and cleaning had been dispensed with, Maryam asked if I could assess what she had prepared thus far. I needed no encouragement! Just to hear her dear voice—from firsthand experience—revisiting the nature of human grief, I wondered if I had, in fact, demanded too much from her. My beloved was, indeed, a princess who had lost her palace only to be found at last with the *hoi polio*—the common folk—and I was one of them! Of more import than this was the loss of our dearly loved only son, David.

I listened, observed, as her notes were shared with me. As

she started to speak her thoughts, I knew without a doubt that Maryam had the inner strength to withstand the sensitive issues that would be exposed during this course. Her own sorrows had prepared her for this counselling role.

'Manaen, I am going to base my major themes on written Scripture and I will need your confirmation of the chosen texts. Here is the initial verse that will set the scene for the whole course (Psalm 23:4):

Though I walk through the valley of death's shadows, I will not fear for You, my Shepherd, are always with me. You guard me with Your rod and You guide me with Your staff and so I am comforted.

I intend to follow these important themes with help from our artist friends. I will ask each to paint a scene that relates to the given subject. Manaen, I have been giving much thought to these aspects of sorrow:

GRIEF HAS ITS SEASON
'Grief comes unbidden and unwanted as a stream of sorrow, a tempest of tears, a mist of mourning, and a silence of sadness. The sun is hidden, shadows give way to gloom, night descends and the chilling winds of winter settle in. The season will take its time and will hold its pain, its loneliness, its lessons in living. But why the anguish? Where is comfort? From whence comes relief?'

GRIEF HAS ITS REASON
'It is in the nature of bereavement—a parting, the loss of companionship, the fracturing of relationships, a wayward son, a departed daughter, a violence, a tragedy— to harbour grief. How does one survive the experience? Why has this happened to me? Where is guidance? What is the remedy?'

GRIEF HAS ITS AVENUES
'Grief will take us on a journey—a journey through the shadows

of sorrow into a renewed dawn. Footprints are to be found along each pathway. The signposts are there but not, it seems, of our choosing. Each avenue may be traversed early or late. Sometimes the maze of anguish or anger, and sometimes the tracks of acknowledgement and acceptance are meant for our feet. Each of these may lead to other paths, running close at hand and not necessarily afterwards! There are always pathways beside a grief path: those of comfort and consolation, courage and confidence, for example. Allow these byways to become highways.'

GRIEF HAS ITS ANSWERS

'All nature lends her wisdom to the parables she speaks to the human soul. Let her speak and allow the Lord to draw near. He is the Valley Guide. He is our Guard in the Gulch. He will hear our personal prayers. With hearts open to receive God's love, we will become aware that He is at work and will bring about the resolution we need.

'You see, Manaen, I listen well.' I smiled the smile of devoted love to her for I realised that Maryam had indeed listened to a series that I had conducted with the believers in Jerusalem following the ascension of Jesus into Heaven. 'Yes, my darling, it is you that provided the outline by which I can safely follow but I realise that the challenges will come in the responses of those who are actually bearing a sorrow.' 'It's there that I may need your help, dear heart. Can we do this thing together?'

'Yes, Maryam, we have shared together, we have grieved together, the Lord will surely be our Guard and Guide. He will guide us through the valleys, He will guard us in the gulches!' We had not been aware that Onesimus had joined our company. There he was, standing in the shadows and, tonight, he had a gentle smile upon his face. Though he said nothing, we knew he was deep in thought.

'Manaen, I plan to map out the course by selecting with care an appropriate text of Scripture that gives rise to a Picture Parable, though of a different ilk to that of your "Initial" series. It's a helpful way to begin. I would then follow its line of reasoning with an introductory comment. It is hoped that my input will open into free and full responses through our discussions and so bring the comfort we desire to those who are sorrowing. When these notes are complete, will you check them for me so that I may be fully prepared for this series of studies?' Maryam is able with ease to read my ready smile of approval. 'Look, Maryam, Onesimus has prepared a supper before we all go to our beds.'

At times, Maryam sought my advice but, mostly, she set herself to the task. Before the week was out, we were able to sit together to scan the parchments she had prepared. It took most of a day to read and ruminate on the content of her work for, at times, the thoughts Maryam had recorded drew forth spontaneous comments and more than once, a lengthy conversation. Actually, we were pleased at this for it meant that the class, also, would find some guidance in Maryam's thoughts. The participants could find that opening up and conversing on a thought provoked by Scripture or the commentary, would help to bring about a resolution of a problematic circumstance.

'Dear one, the course begins next week. Do I have the curriculum in place?' 'Maryam, Let's look at your work just one more time. The basic work is done but let's re-scan the whole. I do not see a problem but let's be sure of all you plan to do. The parchments and their supplied paintings then were lifted one by one. 'Maryam, I would like to also hear your Introductory Comments for each of the topics you have set into the curriculum for this course.' Maryam complied:

GRIEF

Solace in the Psalms
I am drenched with tears, my eyes droop in sorrow... The Lord has heard my cry for mercy, He accepts my plea. (Psalm 6:6-9).

Forest: North Eastern Tasmania

The Picture Parable:
'Rain-drops as tears falling to the earth present a sombre scene. Yet rain and tears have their blessings, too. Rain is for the refreshment of the earth. Tears are for the refreshment of the soul. Both have their healing properties.

After a drought, the farmer and his family feel like dancing in the rain! Tears possess remarkable cleansing qualities and they give relief to pent-up grief. Tears should be given their overflow.

A sorrow acknowledged allows the soul to realise its need of the assistance that's found in The Lord's response to a cry for help.'

Observation:
Clouds weeping in sorrow are a reflection of the God who grieves. He who gave up His Son for us, is not unmindful of our grief.

GRACE

Solace in the Psalms
Keep me safe, O Lord, for in You I take refuge.   (Psalm 16:1–2)

Ballarat, Victoria, Australia

The Picture Parable:
'A vacant seat speaks volumes. It gives the hint of the loss of a loved one, the departure of a friend, or a family member gone with no forwarding address. Emptiness. Vacancy. How does one fill such a space? The vacant chair holds memories long after the parting, or the passing.

Memory is like the bough of a tree hung low to provide a shelter, a mantle of grace. The choicest thing about memories is that they can call to mind the cherished things, the delightful things, the enduring things. In so doing, they can stir the heart to thankfulness in the midst of grief. So, memory is a gift of grace which softens the grief.

Memories can allow the sun to shine on the shadows. The shadows are still there but they are allowed to fall into a new perspective.'

Observation:
God grants a grace that softens death's finality.

DEATH

Solace in the Psalms
O LORD, do not forsake me; be not far from me, O my God. come quickly to help me, O LORD YHVH, my Saviour. (Psalm 38:21, 22).

The Picture Parable:
'The autumn leaf will fall and winter then takes it to the soil. The bare-branched tree will stand bereft, its leafless arms reaching up to the sullen sky.

Winter discourages the flow of life within the tree. But death to the leaves is not the end of the tree. Death is a but comma rather than a full-stop when placed within the context of the greater life of Heaven. The soul lives on past a given span of earthly life.

The tree possesses potential for the coming spring. Full-stops have no place in the grammar of Eternity.'

Loch Lomond, Scotland

Observation:

Bereavement brings the pain of a parting; it may also find the power of a prayer.

MERCY

Solace in the Psalms

To You, O LORD, YHVH, I called; to the LORD I cried for mercy...
Hear, O LORD and be merciful. O LORD, be my help... I will give You
thanks. (Psalm 30:8, 10, 12).

Winter scene, *en route* to Utah, USA

The Picture Parable:

'Chilling mists restrict vision. Dense fog obscures the onward
path. Nimbus clouds can impede our path, yet they may hold the
very grace of God, a mercy for the troubled heart. A lovely word,

mercy. Mercy is not for the sunshine, it's for the shadows. Mercy is for the vulnerable, the defenceless and the oppressed. How may a shadow be a mercy? It certainly can if, in fact, it is the shadow of a shelter near at hand, the shadow of a much-loved friend coming to our aid, or a shadow that allows a grief to be expressed.

A grief cannot be bypassed. It will always show its face, early or late. But some good things can happen in the shadows. It is in the acknowledging of a burdened heart or pain of loneliness that opportunity comes for nature to commence its healing work and renew the will to move on to where the clouds give way to glistening rays of light.'

Observation:
Clouds of grief can be a mercy as they allow space for winter's wounds to heal.

COMFORT

Solace in the Psalms
Even though I walk in the valley of shadows, I will not fear for You are near and You bring Your comfort to me. (Psalm 23:4).

"*In Green Pastures*" Grove, Huon, Tasmania

The Picture Parable:

Comfort is a special word with a wonderful history. In modern parlance, we have managed to weaken the word by emphasising the first syllable: *com*—to be with, beside—and neglecting the second: *fort.* Comfort sits easily with consolation and care. But COM-FORT is best expressed in "to come with strength"!

I am told that, on the night before the events of Calvary, Jesus spoke of the Holy Spirit as the Personification of Comfort! The Greek language contains a wonderful word: *paraclete*. It describes the One who "comes alongside to help"! He is the One who is our Stronghold, our Fort. He is the Source of our inner strength, our fortitude in adversity.'

Observation:

Comfort is the gifting of grace that those who grieve may realise.

STABILITY

Solace in the Psalms

How blessed are the people whose delight is in the Lord... for they shall be like trees planted by streams that bring renewal to us. (Psalm 1:1, 3).

Beckenham, Kent, UK

The Picture Parable:

'No bark can ever hold a tree in place! Skin can never take the place of bone! Bark and skin both have strategic roles to play. The strength of a tree and a person is formed beneath the bark, the skin. It's under the bark, in the soul, that inner fortitude is developed. The winter—be it weather buffeting the tree, or sorrow buffeting the soul—will reveal what the shape of the years and one's circumstance have given to the tree: fallen leaves can no longer shield the tree's condition. And us: fallen defences no longer shield our grief but God is near to bring renewal… Manaen, your tree poem can help us here.' 'I'll have it ready for you.'

THE TREE
O stately tree, with arms uplifted to
The sky as though in worship of the Lord,
You show, upon the clear but winter's day,
A strength within your wood to stand un-awed
By stormy blasts that beat upon your bough:
With foliage flown, you stand unflawed.

You yield to all adversity yet you remain
A forest giant as from the days of old.
I'd take your living secret, steadfast tree,
And send my searching roots down deep to hold
By living faith, life's firmest, surest promises
And raise my arms in prayer to Him, my Lord!

Observation:
As winter's tree reveals its inner strength, a soul immersed in grief may find its stability through trust: spring will come!

ILLUMINATION
Solace in the Psalms
The Lord is close to those whose heart is breaking and He supports

those who are crushed in their soul. Psalm 34:18.

The Picture Parable:
'There is always light beyond the darkest cloud! Even at midnight, the stars shine as brightly as when no cloud obscures their glimmering glory.

Tear-veiled eyes may douse the filtered light of a cloud-hung sun. But give the sun his due: he will rim the darkest cloud in a glorious hint of his presence. In sorrow, filtered light is best. The soul needs its convalescence, it gives time to heal. And, in those shadowed days and nights, the Lord goes about His divine work of soul-renewal. In the deepest night, He comes to bathe the soul in His healing light.'

Sunset, Spencer Gulf, South Australia

Observation:
The darkest cloud of sorrow may hold a hint of glory though the sun is hidden behind the veil of current circumstance.

UNDERSTANDING

Solace in the Psalms
Reveal Your kindness, O LORD, for I am in distress; my eyes grow weak with sorrow. But I trust in You. (Psalm 31:9, 14).

100

The Picture Parable:
'Shadows give shape to stark reality. Look upon the scene on display. You will see a pathway through the forest into the light beyond. In your mind's eye, subtract the shadows. Then:
Where are the trees? Where is the path? Gone, the character, gone the depth, gone the life! This is also a fact in human experience. Take away the shadows, life is no longer realistic. Take away the black and the gold loses its lustre. Where all is sunshine, one finds a desert for there have been no clouds to offer up their showers. The ground, the life, is parched! No rainbows are seen in a parched desert.
Always unwelcome, grief will nonetheless give its textures to the varied scenes of our life. You seek a magnificent portrait of your life? Give to the Master Painter your palette and paintbrush. He knows how to utilise the light and shade. He draws out the stately character that the full palette of life will provide.'

"Facing the Sun" Kangaroo Island, South Australia

Observation:
Shadows may allow the deeper textures of a more profound perspective to emerge. As you face the sun, all the shadows fall behind you. Place them in perspective as you face the challenges of Today.

RESTORATION

Solace in the Psalms
Let the morning announce the news of Your unfailing love and show me the path I should tread, Lord, for I will trust in You. (Psalm 143:8–10).

Stately sentinel, Crabtree, Tasmania

The Picture Parable:
'There can be a world of difference between aloneness and loneliness. While the former may be recognised as a *situation*, the latter may be diagnosed as a *condition*. To be alone is to reside alone. Loneliness, however, is descriptive of feelings. To be lonely is to feel forlorn, isolated, companionless, to be susceptible to sadness.

As the bereaved move on through the process of grieving, there will be a gradual readjustment where the condition of loneliness recedes and acceptance of the changed circumstance allows one to become more accustomed to being alone.

It will take time. But look for the hints of spring. In time, a bud will burst into a blossom. Warmth returns. Listen to the songbirds. Spring is in the air. In time, the human soul is restored again.'

Observation:
God's answer to our grief, our loneliness, our pain, our sorrow, is found in

God's answer to our grief, our loneliness, our pain, our sorrow, is found in renewal and in restoration. It may also be discovered in reconciliation and in reunion. Discern that the time has come to hand over the pain and take delivery of God's grace outpoured on grace.

'And I have an extra Picture Parable to complete this journey through Grief. It will tell its own story, giving rise to conversations about Grace! The crocus will show its shining face to announce that spring is near—we can face the sun again!

Crocus: St James Park, London

'That's the outline, Manaen. No one can prepare adequately for what questions may come, what sorrows may be disturbed, what demands will be placed on me. But, dear heart, I am ready to front up to it. I've cherished this time of reflection and renewal with you. It has helped to clarify my thinking.

'This plan has been born in the afflictions we have known. I see at last that the ways in which we have discerned the hand of the Lord upon our lives has provided the focus for the themes. It has enabled us to at least view the scenes that no doubt we will need to traverse with the participants. We have the route map now. I feel that I am ready at last, to share the shadows and the light that have fallen on the path we have trodden these many years we have lived, loved and learned together.'

'Who would have thought—not even Yehudith and Baruch, my dearly loved *emi* and *abbi*, could have dreamed that here we would be, fulfilling the purposes of my *kebaa-baa-baas*—the "Lamb" in a city far from Bethlehem. Herod the Great would have laughed our childish dreams to oblivion. Yet, here we are. There have been the tragedies among the triumphs. But through all the years, we have traced His hand, proved the power of faith in *Yeshua*-Jesus. He taught us to pray, to trust Him.'

'Oh, that's another thing. I have been asked to present a series on Prayer. It will require much preparation. I must say, though, that John gave me a great idea concerning an absolutely superb means of structuring a theme. I'll endeavour to follow it!'

12. HEIGHT ... DEPTH ... WIDTH

He's back! The "Terror from... " No! No! Not that! Not the "Terror", he's the "Transformed". More than that! Paul: the "Transformer from Tarsus". That's it, I like it! He's back. What a surprise for all the Community of Faith! There we were in our meeting hall, deep in a discussion concerning the need to formalise the expanding social ministry being undertaken by the Church at Antioch when the doors opened. In they walked... Well one of them no more than shuffled in, being the "worse for wear".

Paul and Barnabas, home at last from their great mission; but where was John Mark? Questions would have to wait. Our friends were in need of rest and refreshment. They looked about to drop. We ceased all we were doing to minister to them. We bustled about, brought some drinks, gathered up some food. They barely took a bite. We made them comfortable and waited patiently for them to gather some strength.

Accommodation was arranged and both men were finally allowed to rest and recover the energy required to bring us up to date with their reports.

Paul and Barnabas took a day or two in which to recuperate. Then they came back to us. Both had aged. There was an undercurrent of disquiet in them but they disclosed nothing except their pleasure to be back in Antioch and their joy in the work accomplished during their travels.

'You've already heard of the happenings in Cyprus,' Barnabas declared. 'Apart from the concerns engendered by that sorcerer, the outcome was such a blessing! The warm response of the proconsul, Sergius Paulus, has enabled our witness there to take root!

'We sailed to Perga in Pamphylia, a coastal province of Asia Minor. The struggles associated with our work caused John Mark to leave us. We think that he may have been disappointed when it became obvious to me that a change of leadership was required. Paul was certainly the man better suited to take control of the mission. Or, perhaps it was just homesickness, for Mark returned to Jerusalem. We cannot deny it, the going at times was exceedingly difficult. Mark's immaturity just got the better of him. Paul had taken ill and this compounded the issue of Mark's departure. Paul was disturbed at his defection, to say the least of it.'

Barnabas continued his report. 'It was decided that we should travel into Galatia with very pleasing results, though, as we moved further into the region, we encountered adverse conditions. Upon reflection, we may have moved on too soon for the believers there to become well-grounded in The Faith.

'There is a large Jewish population in Pisidia, the next sector of our Galatian mission. It was some hundred or so miles on from Perga but there was a major roadway and this made our onward journeying quite uneventful. You may be aware that this is a major Roman Colony with all the attendant privileges.'

Still struggling with some unaccountable health problems, Paul took up the reporting at this stage, giving emphasis to his major message: 'I was not neglecting the Gentile world into which we are carrying the Gospel. However, the Jewish synagogue was an obvious setting in which to make a commencement. Well steeped in The Law, surely the message of salvation would be received warmly. And, as it was customary for visiting rabbis to be given opportunity to speak, here was my forum!

'I spoke the Gospel with my usual fervour and it was pleasing to have the congregation approach us following the meeting to request that I speak again on the following Sabbath. Many followed us as we proceeded to our lodgings. Questions were asked and our answers appeared to be most satisfactory to them. We urged these people to continue in the grace of God.

'Things got quite out of hand as we made our way to the synagogue on that second Sabbath. It seemed as though the entire population was turning out to see what we would say that day. The Jews were not amused and made it plain to all! I spoke most forthrightly to the infuriated Jews explaining that it had been our plan to share the Gospel with them as they were our priority. "But, as you have no desire to hear our news and prefer to close your ears to any thought of receiving the gift of Eternal Life through Jesus Christ, we will turn now to the Gentile world! Know this, however, we came in response to God's Call:
I have chosen you to bring Light to the Gentiles so that salvation may be extended to the whole world. Know your own Scripture! Look at, consider, Isaiah 49:6".

'The Gentiles clapped their hands with joy! The Jews incited leading citizens to stir up such persecution that we were forced to leave the city. As we were expelled, we let the Jews know of our disgust by shaking off the dust of that city from our shoes.'

Barnabas took up the narrative to explain the happenings in Iconium—the next city on their mission plan. 'Our work was so effective that many believed. This did not please the Jews who stirred up trouble. A plot was foiled by our hasty departure for

Lystra and Derbe. Things took a startling turn at Lystra for Paul was able—in the power of the Holy Spirit—to make a crippled man stand on his feet, healed! The city was enraptured! The citizens treated us like gods. Can you believe it? Me: the great god *Zeus*?! And Paul, obviously the teacher: *Hermes*, no less!

'This had to be stopped! We rushed into the midst of the thronging, adulating crowd. "Stop! Stop! We are men just like yourselves. But we have come to share some extraordinary news!" We shared the Gospel then. Still, it was all we could do to stop them bowing and scraping to us! Then it happened, of course. Some Jews arrived from Iconium spreading a propaganda of their own.

'Their vitriol then turned the accolades of the crowds into a denunciation. Some agitators took up stones and hurled them at Paul.' Barnabas paused, quite emotional now. He then resumed. 'Paul was dragged from the city, presumably dead. But there were some who had believed the truth of the Gospel and followed on behind. When it was safe for them, these new friends lifted him and brought him back into the city.

'As it was too dangerous to remain in Lystra, safe passage was arranged for us to journey on to Derbe where a large number of people chose to believe the Gospel. We then returned the way we had come. It was so important to display our confidence to the converts that the Lord is with us in all our endeavours. We would not allow hardship or peril to deter us from our work. And that was the message we shared with the faithful souls who welcomed us back to their cities so wholeheartedly.

'In thinking about all that was achieved during this great mission, the likes of which have never been attempted before, we humbly give our thanks to the Lord who has sustained us throughout the pilgrimage!

'You will have noticed that Paul—no, forgive me, Paul—Paul has not quite recovered from the ordeal of that stoning at Lystra.

His wounds are not yet healed and he will need time and medical assistance to bring about a full recovery.'

It was our turn to bring good news to Barnabas and Paul! A room had been set up some months ago by Nicolas, our Social Services Manager, for Maryam and her two assistants—yes, Eustace and Angela, the newly marrieds—to provide a service of physical therapy to any who had no means of paying doctors to assist in their recovery. Eustace went at once to Paul who knew immediately that here was a man dedicated to the needs of the less fortunate—of whom he was definitely one at that time! Paul was now beginning to sense an easing of his pain.

Maryam was on hand to cleanse any open wounds and, in our sharing at the end of the day, my beloved told me of the shocking lesions Paul had sustained. It broke her heart to realise that our only son, David, had been felled—assassinated—by just one rock, flung so belligerently during that Jerusalem stoning. Only the Lord could have saved Paul from a like fate! Maryam would do all that she could to aid Paul's return to health. But it would take some time for him to recover.

I was later to reflect upon the clarification of the news concerning John Mark and it caused me to give serious consideration to the decision-making processes of those who are standing at a "cross road" where life-determining directions must be decided. Which way? God's way? My way? How does one decide? My writing kit was called again into service that night.

13. CROSS ROADS

The queries that rise within my soul most often send me into the rhythms of a soliloquy where the mind gives expression to a quandary, and proceeds to travel along the avenues of thought in search of an answer which would calm the troubled soul. John

Mark's dilemma pressed hard upon me. I realised that Maryam and I had reached a "cross road" in our own life-journey. We had chosen the right road for, here we are, emersed in such soul-satisfying tasks which bear the imprimatur of the Lord's own choosing. And, there was the "Terror from Tarsus". There was John bar Zebedee... Yes! Of course! We all of us will reach a "cross road" which has the potential for life-changing consequences.

I must pray for John Mark. I must pray for Onesimus! And now, my pen must be pushed across the parchment to bring its own exclamations to my thoughts:

AT THE CROSS ROADS
Tune : *Hardy Norseman* C.M.

I'm standing at the cross roads, Lord,
Which way, the way for me?
There is no sign except this cross,
What could its challenge be?

'Take up your cross,' the Lord declares.
'And follow Me today;
I'll tread the future's path with you,
My Light will show the way.'

I've scanned the pleasant scenes of Earth,
The choice is mine you see;
Where is there ease upon this way,
The road to Calvary?

I'm weighing up the circumstance:
Which way, the worthy way?
Is there no better consequence?
What is His will for me?

He bids me not to think of cost,
The greater good to find;

But could I walk His cross-bound way,
My will with His aligned?

I'll take the challenge offered me,
This path will not deprive;
Christ walked the Calvary road for me,
He leads me into life.

'Amen', I thought, as I packed my writing kit away.

The Church Council at Antioch—including Paul and Barnabas who had been leading members before their epic missionary journey—was meeting to discuss the possibility of establishing a special ministry to the youth of the city. Many teenagers and folk in their early twenties were seeking to become more involved in the work of the Church and it was our desire to harness their hopes, set them securely on the Path of Life and assist them by encouraging them to fulfil their highest aspirations. I was excited about the prospects and offered a suggestion that I thought would assist the introduction of this worthy enterprise.

Demetrius is a *paidagogos* or—as we would be more prone to say, a pedagogue and using the incorrect term "teacher" for the person so designated. Demetrius is not actually a school teacher, he is more precisely, a school guide—a guardian, if you like—whose responsibility it is to conduct a child or youth to and from school, to oversight the general behaviour of the youngster and to provide tutoring where possible. The pedagogue is attendant to the needs of the child in his care. I knew that Demetrius was a young man of blameless character and would be ideal as a youth leader in the Church at Antioch. The Council agreed wholeheartedly. Demetrius was approached and was thoroughly delighted with the extra responsibility given into his hands!

Much time was given by us all in the ensuing days to prepare

Demetrius for his onerous task. He did not appear overawed by the possibilities now facing him. His training as a pedagogue would stand him in good stead. The Church Council is prepared to give support and counsel whenever required. We will stand by him and the program he will prepare and then present to the youth of the Church. When announced during the following Sunday Worship Service, the news was met with loud hurrays! Demetrius would receive great support and assistance from Astrid, the young woman to whom he is promised.

The youth responded with alacrity and soon there were hikes into the surrounding countryside, games nights, quiz nights, music nights, practical service opportunities, quality living discussions, and a camping caper is being arranged for a Summer Saturday-cum-Sunday, that latter day being given over to worship in the wild, followed by a study of the teaching of the Church. What delighted me about the leadership that Demetrius is giving to the youth of the Church is that he has formed a friendship with Onesimus. For so long, our young charge appeared aimless as to his future but the youth program has caught his imagination and he is showing a distinct interest in the program, occasionally participating with satisfied sentiment.

Amid all this exhilarating activity, I was hard put to find adequate time to prepare for the forthcoming series on prayer that had been requested by the Church as a whole. I had formed the opinion that John bar Zebedee's excellent "7" structuring of the book he is in the process of writing, concerning the life and teaching of *Yeshua*–Jesus, would give a most helpful guideline for my own structuring of the impending series on prayer. In the years of my spiritual pilgrimage, I had absorbed much from my own experiences of praise, but also of petition and the like!

The figure 7 appeals to me as a means of covering the many nuances of the prayer experience most adequately. It's time that I began to formulate the plans. Once commenced, all the major aspects of the theme came together quite effectively:

THE PRAYER EXPERIENCE

THE FORMS OF PRAYER
1 ADORATION   Realisation of the Glory of the Lord
2 PRAISE   Recognising the Greatness of the Lord
3 THANKSGIVING   Responding to the Generosity of the Lord
4 INTERCESSION   Reckoning on the Grace of the Lord
5 PETITION   Reaching for the Giving of the Lord
6 DEDICATION   Responding to the Goal of the Lord
7 ACQUIESCENCE   Rejoicing in the Governance of the Lord

THE SENSES OF PRAYER
1 HEAR   Impetus of Scriptural truth
2 SEE   Insights gained through Creation
3 TOUCH   Intensity of the Hand of God on one's life
4 TASTE   Imbibing of "soul food"
5 SMELL   Infusion of the Breath of God's Spirit
6 THE "SIXTH" SENSE   Illumination of the soul in God's Presence
7 "BEYONDNESS"   Identification with the Lord in communion

THE EXPRESSIONS OF PRAYER
1 STILLNESS   Be still and know I AM, *Yahweh*–LORD
2 WORDS   Be ready to tell what is on the mind
3 MEDITATION   Be able to cast aside all distractions
4 BEING   Be ready to recognise "The Presence"
5 LITURGY   Be a ready participant in prepared wording
6 EXTEMPORARY   Be able to say what is in the heart
7 SONG   Be attuned: melodic poetry speaks for you

THE PROBLEMS WITH PRAYER
1 BUSYNESS   Never be too busy to "stay" awhile
2 OBSTRUCTIONS   Never allow obstacles to impede prayer
3 DOUBTS   Never let the negative blur the positive
4 UNWORTHINESS   Never count yourself as not good enough

5	LANGUAGE	Never let lack of fluency impede prayer
6	SUBJECTS	Never consider anything outside God's care
7	FOCUS	Never let peripheries interfere with focus

THE REASONS FOR PRAYER

1	OTHERS' NEEDS	There's always one who needs your prayer
2	REQUESTS	The Lord listens, responds: Yes! No! Wait!
3	QUIET TIME	The time given to prayer is renewal time
4	NURTURE	The gift of prayer is a growth in grace
5	GUIDANCE	There is no one without a need of guidance
6	PEACE	The peace of God surpasses understanding
7	TRYST	The daily meeting with God is vital

THE ARENAS OF PRAYER

1	SANCTUARY	The Convening Place
2	QUIET PLACE	The Contentment Place
3	MINISTRY	The Challenging Place
4	COMPANY	The Communicating Place
5	PERIL	The Crucial Place
6	CIRCUMSTANCE	The Consoling Place
7	COMMITMENT	The Contracting Place

THE RESULTS OF PRAYER

1	ACKNOWLEDGEMENT	The Lord has heard my prayer
2	REALISATION	The joy of being in the presence of God
3	PEACE	The results of prayer are in God's hands
4	IMPETUS	The inner urge to serve is acted on
5	STRENGTHENING	The mighty reinforcement of God's Spirit
6	THANKFULNESS	The gratitude of a soul blessed by grace
7	RESOLUTION	The resolve to place myself in God's will

············

I'll know the time to insert the appropriate segment of "AWARENESS"—the product of my writing kit—by the input of discussion and of actual prayer as the themes evolve! I place it here so that I may keep its content well in mind:

CROSS ROADS

AWARENESS

THE SEVEN SENSES OF PRAYER

I HEAR the tenor of Your tread,
Your timely footfall coming on
The shining ray of dawn's first light.
You gently call my name into
The moment of awakening
And now I wait to know once more
The calming cadence of Your voice.
I come with heart made mellow now
For You have come to meet my need;
I bow in homage to Your love ...

Now, Lord.

I SEE Your hand of providence!
Relying on Your promises,
Rejoicing in Your faithfulness,
I speak my heartfelt thankfulness
Into the dawn's pure light of grace.
Here You illumine me and all
My earthly sight recedes from this,
The greater glow of Heaven's Face.
This is Your holy ground on which
I stand to bring my offering ...

Here, Lord.

I TOUCH the landscape of Your love,
The territory of prayer's expanse.
In reaching for Your warm embrace,
I find that You have stooped to me,
Reached down to me, enfolded me!
You walk with me, You guide my path
Via meditation's avenues.
On mountain heights, in shadowed vales,
You both precede and follow me

CROSS ROADS

And give Your hand when rough the road ...
Thanks, Lord.

I TASTE the pleasures of Your fare
Provision for my sustenance,
As I receive Your broken bread
Prepared upon the sacred page.
Your promises, and plans, and prods,
Enrich my life in truth expressed.
Sincere, the milk of Your blessed word
That, for my day, brings glowing health
To heart and soul so hungry for
The Bread of Life, the Gift of Love ...

My Lord.

A FRAGRANCE redolent of Heaven
Alerts the mind to focussed thought,
Eternity in touch with time
Brings, wafting on the Spirit's Breath,
Aromas with such pungent joy
That seep into the depths of soul
To stir the core of wonderment.
Your perfumed promises released,
Infusing all my life with hope,
The Breath of Life brings Heaven near ...

Stay, Lord.

BY INTUITION, insight gleaned,
I sense Your listening ear bent low,
Your counsel and Your comfort now.
As always, grace preceded me,
Your loving arms encompassed me
Across the doubtful span of days,
The nights of pain without relent,
Until Your solace came. Within
This sanctuary I spread my pleas

And intercede for Earth's grim need ...

O Lord.

I SENSE an ecstasy beyond
Quintessence in enraptured streams
Like dancing waters running deep.
Emotion's swelling tide now sweeps
As waves upon the nearer shore
Of conscious thought in vibrant prayer.
Within this surge Earth's sense is seeped
As Spirit sings to spirit here.
You bathe my wounds, my heart is healed;
Your counsel mine, Your will my will ...

Yes, Lord.

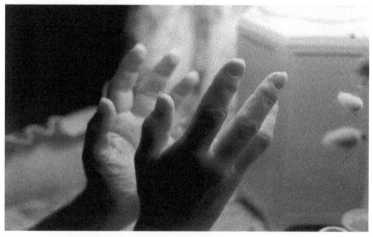

"Enlightenment", at home: The Avenue, Melbourne

13. "HELP!"

'There will need to be an investigation. Is Demetrius able to give an account today?' Ambrose, the leader of the Church Council inquired. Having seen and spoken with the young man, who was still struggling through the after-effects of the traumatic events associated with the ill-fated camping expedition, I advised another day, at least. I could not speak for Astrid. The news concerning her would now need to wait for Demetrius' report. I advised against an inquisition. The better plan would be to arrange some seating by the open fire in the meeting hall to emphasise an informal gathering. This would ease the evident and understandable distress of Demetrius.

Following his morning duties as pedagogue, Demetrius fronted up to the Church Council the next day. 'You are looking very pale, young man. Do you feel that you can relate, today, those dreadful happenings at the camp?' 'Yes, Ambrose, I'm rested now and it will be good to be able to explain it all. Everything was proceeding according to plan and everyone had entered wholeheartedly into every excursion. It all happened in the early evening. The shadows in the forest obscured its approach. It latched on to Astrid before anyone was aware of its presence.

'What latched on?' 'Oh, it was a viper. Not large at all but carrying enough venom to take Astrid's life. Onesimus rushed up, commanded that I take off my belt.' 'Your belt, Demetrius?' 'That's what I wondered, too, Ambrose.' "No time to explain. Quick, give it to me," he said, using it as a tourniquet. I pleaded, "Look at her leg, Onesimus! It's swelling, turning blue." "Astrid, darling, don't die. Please, don't die." Onesimus then spoke firmly to me. He said, "Have faith! That's what Pastor Pa would say!" Then, "A sharp knife, take a sharp bladed knife, run it through the flames and then into the ewer of pure water to cool it down.

Bring it to me. Hurry now! Her life depends on it." 'I ran at once, took the knife, heated it, cooled it, gave it to Onesimus who commanded that two young women hold Astrid still on the ground, by her shoulders.

'Ambrose, everyone: Onesimus gashed Astrid's leg, right near the point of the viper's puncture marks! Blood spurted out!

"What are you doing?" I asked frantically, looking at Onesimus who was suddenly stilled. He answered so very calmly that I wondered at his attitude. But, more than that, what had he done? The blood still flowed but not so freely as at first. Then it gave up its bid for freedom!'

"Demetrius, take off your head-band!" 'My head-band?' "Yes, at once. Take it to that pot of water boiling on the coals. Dip it in, all of it! Lift it by those tongs and carry it back to me. It will have cooled enough by then."

'Gentlemen, he then began to wind my head-band into a bandage about Astrid's leg. The blood had ceased its flow. Onesimus then explained that, once the blood had been staunched, the poison had drained away. But the wound must be kept away from all grit and grime. It must be kept pure until it was healed. He handed back my belt then and Astrid was freed from the grip of her friends.

'The worst of it was past. I took a deep breath and then asked Onesimus how on earth he knew what to do. For some reason, he became quite hesitant but said, "I saw a doctor do this once. It is not something that one easily forgets."

'As you know, Astrid is recovering in the clinic room. Maryam and her team are taking good care of her. I saw her walking with an under-the-shoulder wooden frame this morning. My relief is beyond words. Pastor Pa (taking up the Onesimus terminology), do you realise that he saved Astrid's life? Astrid and I will be indebted to him all our lives.'

It was my turn to speak. I found it difficult to be in any way articulate. Onesimus had actually commanded, 'Have Faith!' This was a turning point in his view of the Christian faith! He had been listening! He had been observing! He had been considering! Onesimus was walking towards a personal belief in Christ! And something else, he is showing great potential. He has taken over a traumatic event with skill and a confidence not found overnight!

Upon his return home with all the campers that Sunday night, Onesimus had not disclosed his intervention in that life-or-death situation. There was no, 'Guess what I did, Pastor Pa,' no 'I saved Astrid's life, Pastor Pa!' Onesimus was revealing a maturity beyond his years. What would the future hold for him?

A day or two later, when I sensed an appropriate moment, I dared to ask Onesimus what he knew about faith. What does it mean to be a person who is prepared to accept a truth although there was no visible accounting as to its authenticity? I endeavoured to allow him to speak rather than do any guiding of the conversation. But I find it difficult not to rush into an empty moment!

'Faith can be seen, Pastor Pa!' 'How come? If you see a thing, you don't have to struggle to accept its existence.' 'Well, I see the effects of faith in you and Mother Emi. I listen to what you say and I am pleased to say that what you say—ha ha—makes sense for you say it best not in your words but in your deeds!' Well, that staggered me! I took some time to recover.

In gathering my breath, I managed at last to ask the all-important question. 'Onesimus, Mother Emi and I are so pleased to see that you really feel at home with the Church Community now. Have you been able to give any consideration to actually committing your way to the Lord? Could you decide to become a Christian?' 'I cannot do that, Pastor Pa, no matter how much I would desire it to be so.'

'You cannot? Would it really be so difficult?' 'There would be no difficulty at all. I hold the truth of it in my mind. The thing is, I cannot allow that truth to sink into my heart, my soul, as you would put it.' Again, he staggered me! I gasped his name. I held his hand. I chose to ask, 'Have I not explained the nature of one's commitment to Christ in a manner that is understandable or acceptable to you?' 'Oh, yes, you have! I do believe, but I cannot receive...' There were no words that I could pull together that would deal with this impasse in any way effectively. So, I merely looked at him.

Onesimus then made the matter clear and plain to me. 'Pastor Pa, if I were to commit my life to Christ, I would need to own up to my past. I cannot do that. It would be the end of me! My life is here. I will support you and the Church at Antioch to the best of my ability. You can depend on me. But do not ask of me what I am unable to do.' I nodded then, accepting the reason for his dilemma and I loved him even more deeply then.

As good and better than his word, Onesimus swung into action at the Church. His meritorious deed at the recent camp had earned him a place of honour among the Community of Faith. Onesimus was given due respect. And besides, his meals are memorable! Yes, he took on the heavy duties of the cook in our ever-expanding area of social services. It seemed a natural place for him. I began to think that, in his previous service—or slavery, I think, more to the point—this young man had already learned the art of mixing up some dishes to tempt the tastebuds of us all!

Astrid was moving about with greater ease and it was of no surprise to me that she came with Demetrius to our home so soon after her near demise. Maryam busied herself preparing a meal adequate for a larger clientele that night. It was not really of any necessity that they should explain their visit for their shining faces made their intent quite plain to us all.

Astrid's recent experience brought their shared desire to the fore. 'Manaen, Pastor Pa—as Onesimus would say—we wish to be married in the same manner as Eustace and Angela. Could you arrange this for it is our desire that you would be the celebrant.' I responded with a hearty, 'Certainly I will!'

A parchment was then laid out upon the table so that the couple's best desires and promises could be recorded for use on their wedding day. 'Oh, Pastor Pa'—the appellation had certainly caught on within the Community and I saw no reason to douse the sentiment—'we have thought most keenly about the content of our promises and we can think of no additions necessary to the worthy and blessed vows of Eustace and Angela. Is it possible that we could speak those same lines? We have asked permission from them both. They seem more than pleased to comply.' How delighted I was to agree.

'Are there any particular requirements that we should include in the Wedding Service?' 'Oh, would you write a song for us with Bernice to add a melody which Maryam could sing?' 'I'll ask my writing kit to obey,' I offered with a touch of humour that brought some laughter to the room.

Astrid then declared that she would like very much for her friend Daphne to assist her down the aisle in the meeting hall. Demetrius chimed in with, 'I want Onesimus to stand with me as my best friend. He could then partner Daphne during the ensuing feast. Yes, I know he is the cook but I'm sure there are some able assistants who can take over for the night.' 'You can ask him now.' 'Onesimus, we need your presence here!' It was all arranged and we were able, finally, to bid our visitors a late 'Good night' before turning to our beds.

The next morning found me sitting at my desk with the able writing kit about to do my bidding as an inspiration came that would fit the theme so apparent for the wedding.

WEDDING VOWS

(Tune: *Mozart* 8.8.8.8.8.8. Iambic)

O Lord, You call us to this day
That we may celebrate with joy,
The offering of hand and heart
Within this hallowed sanctuary:
May now the sharing of love's vows
Be sealed in perfect harmony.

Within this consecrated hour,
We join in prayer before Your Face:
Wellspring of Joy, O Fount of Life,

Our strength is in Your gifted peace;
Out from amazing depths of love,
There flows a constant stream of grace.

In every promise of Your word,
We rest secure and lift our praise.
Spirit Divine, with us abide,
Indwell, sustain and strengthen us;
We seek Your blessing as we pray,
Now guide us, Lord, through all our days.

Rejoicing in this hour we know
The pattern of the love You wove
Into the fabric of our lives:
It's bonded by Your grace to prove
How precious are Your ways! O Lord,
Entwine with peace our joy, our love.

When the wording was completed, I asked the couple to read the song through in order to gain their blessing on the contribution to the occasion. My song became a hymn, a prayer, as Maryam and Bernice brought a fitting conclusion to the service. As the celebrant, I was more than moved to hear my own beloved of our many years of mutual love expressing so wonderfully well the words that had been dedicated for the wedding of Demetrius and Astrid.

It was with a great deal of satisfaction that I observed a growing rapport between Onesimus and the Apostle Paul. Taking into account his momentous mission into Galatia, perhaps Paul could bring into the life of this young man a confidence in the future that I, as yet, have been unable to engender within him. I could only hope. In the meantime, trouble was brewing!

15. AN ICY BLAST

Some visitors from Jerusalem turned up. The men were, indeed, believers but also, Pharisees! Such men were well versed in assessing the state of affairs pertaining to belief and practice. They became alarmed that the Church at Antioch was condoning the inclusion of men and boys in our Community of Faith who dared to claim belief in Christ and act accordingly without, at first, agreeing to undertake the rigid rule of the Jewish way of doing things!

No man or boy could claim allegiance to the Lord without at first undergoing that minor surgical removal of the unmentionable—to Greek minds—foreskin! The brethren at Antioch were incensed! The Greeks were on the verge of, literally, turning their backs on the whole ridiculous assumption that a physical snip could make the difference in a spiritual transaction! They would have none of it. I could not blame them. The possibility was raising its ugly head that the Church would revert into a minor Jewish sect and forsake its mission to the whole world!

I had seen, many years ago, that the Jewish custom of circumcision—so appropriate in those ancient desert wanderings when hygiene was at less than its best—could in no way make a person right with God. Paul—once the "Terror from Tarsus", a Pharisee of the Pharisees—now stood up for the Church. He put the matter plainly:

THE JUST SHALL LIVE BY FAITH THROUGH GRACE!

'Faith is not to be found at the point of a surgeon's scissors! Faith is a matter of soul scissors: the cutting out of sin from the life by the sacrificial death of Jesus Christ! The Lord has made known what He thinks of the matter: He has gifted these Gentiles—with or without the cutting—with the Holy Spirit. He is pleased with us and, them! I ask you now, why are you so keen to lift up the yoke of servitude that the Lord has removed from our backs and place it there once more so that freedom to serve is replaced by an imperative to serve?'

The altercation became so sharp it was determined that a delegation should travel to Jerusalem to sort out the issue once and for all. I declined the request to accompany them lest Herod hear of it and hasten my demise! Paul and Barnabas led the group and the power of their persuasive argument was such that James, the leader of the Jerusalem Church, stood to declare the final determination of the Council:

'There is no reason for the Jerusalem Church to place such a burden upon the lives of Gentiles who have come to faith in Christ by the merits of His grace. Why make their daily walk of faith more difficult? We should be applauding them! It has been decided that a letter be prepared to give this ruling—with the proviso that certain matters of sexual morality, an embargo on idol worship, and the proper preparation of meat should be observed in all decency.'

The whole Council was in agreement and decided to send two of their members—Judah and Silas—back to Antioch with

Paul and Barnabas. The reading of the letter brought unbounded joy to the brethren at Antioch. It was pleasing in particular to note the reaction of our Greek brothers. The problem was solved and our Church is the better, the stronger, for the debate and its most sensible conclusion!

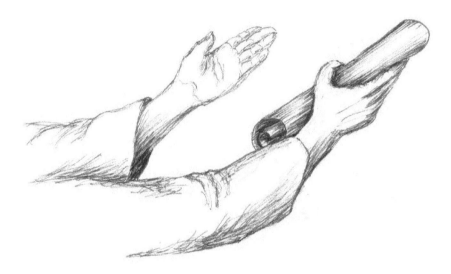

I must say that I am impressed by young Silas! And Paul agrees with me! The recent discussions I have enjoyed with Paul have caused me, unaccountably, to remember the years of our association in Jerusalem—in particular, my classroom altercations at the Rabbinic School with the "Terror from Tarsus". What a remarkable change has taken place. I have commented on Paul's transformation but I, Manaen ben Baruch, have also experienced the transformation that is the outcome of what can only be called a "re-birth".

In fact, that is exactly how *Yeshua*–Jesus referred to the event when He came to visit Maryam and me in Jerusalem. Nicodemus was also our honoured guest on that never-to-be-forgotten night. 'You must be born again if you are to enter the Kingdom of Heaven,' Jesus said. 'Born again? That's impossible, Rabbi,' Nicodemus remarked with astonishment. Though quite taciturn, I had thought the same!

'I speak of a re-birth in the soul,' Jesus replied—or, words to that effect. 'Spiritual birth requires the inbreathing of the Holy Spirit. The physical birth is that of water—as any midwife can verify. That which is spiritual is born of the Spirit.' 'How can that be possible?' It was my turn to speak: 'His reply was unforgettable. 'The wind blows where it will. You will recognise its presence by the movement of a tree in the breeze, but you cannot tell from whence it comes nor where it will go. So is everyone who is born of the Holy Spirit.'" (John 3:1–21).

Memory is a precious gift and it allows one to "travel" down the corridors of the mind where it is possible to glean the learnings of past experience. Such was happening today as I recalled not only that wonderfully illuminating evening where Nicodemus dared to ask the question, "How can one be born again?" but later occasions where new truth flooded my soul. I made notes as thoughts came, with a few sketches to set these seven symbols of the Holy Spirit not only in my mind but also in my writing kit's files!

I was revisiting this conversation with Paul who became quite animated and proceeded to tell me of some encounters he and Barnabas had experienced in Galatia as so many people came to accept the Lord as Saviour of their lives. Paul then shared his disquiet regarding current mission enterprises.

'I am concerned for the believers in Galatia. News is reaching me that all is not well in their fledgling churches in that region. I am composing a treatise that I intend to place in the hands of a courier so that my concerns may be felt by those who, at the beginning, ran so well but now seem to have run out of spiritual energy. I think they need another "inbreathing" by the Holy Spirit. May I run some of my ideas by you? Your wisdom may cast some calm across my troubled waters.' I agreed, of course!

'Manaen, I want to reiterate that there is no other Gospel than the Good News Barnabas and I presented to the Galatians on our mission journey among them. How can they turn so quickly from the truth we brought to them? This Gospel is no invention of a human mind! It is the Gospel that is read in the life of the Son of God who surrendered himself so that the world may turn from its darkness into the Light!

'I intend to remind the Galatians of my wicked persecution of all who dared to believe in Jesus, how He met with me, changed my life and how He called me to be His ambassador to the Gentile world.' I responded then by remarking on a miracle so dramatic that all the believers saw its effect in Paul's life and accepted the turn-around. 'It was enough to strengthen our own faith by the observation of your new-found faith and its effectiveness!'

'The real issue, Manaen, is: are they going to become slaves to "Thou shalt not!" or accept the freedom of "the just who live by faith"? Oh, if only they could realise that now faith has come, there is no need to rely on The Law. Laws can only point out where we can go wrong without offering a means to make things right. Faith makes things right for the Christian maxim says just this: Love God and do what you like!' 'Now that is a great "turn around" from the once "Terror from Tarsus". You'll have to explain yourself even to me!' 'Oh Manaen: "Love God and do what you like" is easy. The crux of the matter is: if you really love the Lord, what you *like* to do is seek His ways, follow His commands, and live to serve Him come what may.' I laughed a joyous laugh, slapped him on the back and thanked him for the depth of his perception!

'Manaen, it is my desire to encourage the Galatians to live according to the guidance of the Holy Spirit. If they will allow themselves to be led by the Spirit, they will no longer find themselves in the straightjacket of The Law for their original sinful nature has been crucified—a good description of re-birth.

'I do not intend to close my letter until I point out something that pertains to the spiritual nourishment that is gained by our reliance upon the Holy Spirit. There is an abundance of "spiritual fruit" by which the Spirit sustains and strengthens us. The more we rely on the Spirit, the more He can rely on us! This can lead into some comments of a practical nature regarding the various types of "fruit"! This letter is of vital importance. It's as good as I can do: my only boast is in Jesus Christ! (Galatians 5:22–23).

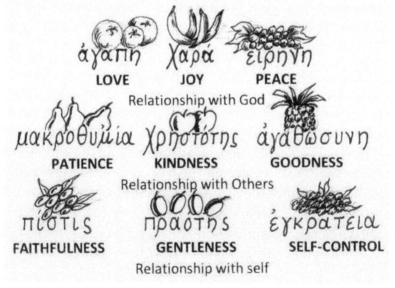

ἀγάπη — LOVE Χαρά — JOY εἰρήνη — PEACE

Relationship with God

μακροθυμία — PATIENCE χρηστότης — KINDNESS ἀγαθωσυνη — GOODNESS

Relationship with Others

πίστις — FAITHFULNESS πραοτης — GENTLENESS ἐγκρατεια — SELF-CONTROL

Relationship with self

16. RETURN TO THE CROSS ROADS

'What's that? John Mark? You say he has arrived back in Antioch? Amazing. Where is he? Oh, he's lodging with Barnabas. I'll go to him.' Closing up my writing kit, I donned an outer cloak and, after bidding farewell to Maryam, I made my way through the bustling market crowds and was soon knocking on the familiar door. I was pleased to see that it was Mark who opened up and welcomed me inside.

Barnabas seemed particularly contented with life in general! And Mark? He had matured—at least, he gave every indication this was so. 'Welcome back, Mark. We have missed you. Tell me, what is the situation in Jerusalem? Your parents? What of Nicodemus?'

'Wow, one question at a time, Manaen. Let's take the last one first. I have no recent news of Nicodemus. He has had to lie low. He is considered to be an insurrectionist as he no longer toes the party line, so to speak. The Sanhedrin was not amused by his forthright approval of The Nazarene. It has been said that he condemned the detestable actions of Annas and Caiaphas in the Sanhedrin. Indeed, he had every right to do so. He's elderly now, of course. Perhaps, today, he is conversing with his crucified Lord and Saviour in Heaven.'

'Indeed. We may never discover his whereabouts. Nicodemus was my mentor. He instilled within me the very best of Hebrew Heritage. I will always be grateful. But do go on. Your *em*, how is she now? How has your *abba* fared through all the upheaval in the city?'

It was heart-warming to hear of the good in the midst of the tumultuous times those of faith living in Jerusalem were experiencing. And, as I reflected on the history bound up in the walls of that great city, I thought of the living history that people such as John Mark held in their memories and in their soul. I remembered also that conversation with the Apostle John who had pointed out the good sense of discovering a young man capable of recording the history of the birth of Christianity in an action-packed, youthful style. Such an accounting would need to be accomplished from first hand, eye-witness observations. Here is our man!

'Mark, I understand that you have an interest in recording stories—you were educated in the Temple's Rabbinic School. I have a project for you, at least, for you to think about. I am aware that you actually saw many of the events associated with the life of *Yeshua*–Jesus. I know that the Last Supper was held in the upper room in your home and that you followed the Lord and His disciples down that dreadful route to Gethsemane. Could you pull together those memories and record them for posterity? John—that is, the apostle—and I are hoping to commence the production of a *New Testament*. None of the history of those momentous events must be lost after we pass on.'

Mark's face said it all before any reply was forthcoming. Mark thought it was a grand idea. He nodded his head vigorously in the affirmative then said, 'I have spent much time with the Apostle Peter and hope to meet up with him again one day. I know that he would be able to fill in all the missing facts. He could keep me on track. I've already recorded some memorable occasions and these notes will give me an early start.'

'What are your plans, Mark?' 'I am hopeful of being involved once more in the specially challenging work of a missionary. I know the ropes, well, some of them. It became imperative to gain some respite from all the toil and strife associated with that first venture. I found it necessary to leave Barnabas and Paul so soon after having set out on that epic journey.' I saw the creases of concern steal over the benign features of Barnabas. What would Paul think of this? Could he condone Mark's second bite at service? We were soon to find out!

'Never! The lad is a liability!' 'But Paul, he's back. He knows what would be expected of him. He knows the way we work. He's happy to return to us.' 'No way! I cannot abide the thought of him wandering off again at the slightest hint of an obstruction on the road. I will not have it so!' Barnabas continued to plead the cause of his repentant relative but Paul was adamant. The argument was sharp. Paul refused to yield his ground and, in the end of it, there was a parting of the ways. Barnabas and his able assistant—John Mark—chose to return to Cyprus where they could continue the good work started there at the commencement of that first remarkable journey into "all the world". Well, it wasn't far but it was a start and, thanks to Sergius Paulus, it was a good start. Barnabas and Mark were welcomed back and they sank themselves into the somewhat fragile ministry on that island realm.

From where I sit—and I am more eager to sit than stand these days—it was possible to take a reasonable stock of the situation. Barnabas is gone from us. Somewhat more mature than Paul in years, I think that perhaps he would be no longer able to keep pace with Paul who is a man driven to succeed on his mission. His team would have, at times, great difficulty in sustaining the rigours required of them.

I have the greatest regard for Barnabas, a friend now of some years. The contribution he made to the early days of Church expansion cannot be over-estimated. He was a generous man, warm, friendly and ready to spend and be spent for the Faith to which he displayed a devotion that was so very commendable. If it had not been for the kindness of Barnabas, Paul may never have been acceptable to the Church leaders in Jerusalem. Barnabas introduced Paul to the brethren in Antioch and it was from there—with the backing of our Church—the two had set out with John Mark to conquer the world for Christ! Paul owes so much to Barnabas. Will he ever come to an acknowledgement of that debt he surely owes to his friend? As someone has said, 'Barnabas is a good man. He is a man filled with Holy Spirit power and of vibrant faith.' And I concur.

And what of Paul? He was not deterred. He was fully determined to return to the scenes of his earlier journey. He came to me yesterday with some rather startling but welcome news. Paul has asked Silas—yes, the young man who had journeyed to Antioch with the delegation that had so successfully put their case on behalf of the Gentiles—to accompany him. Silas is certainly a good choice: he is a Roman citizen, as is Paul. This status will provide a certain amount of security as they move about uncharted territory. People do not easily confront a Roman citizen without fear and trepidation! Another aspect that gives a further point in his favour is that Silas—as a member of the Jerusalem Church—could be more acceptable to Jews still inclined to hold to the strictures of The Law! Actually, Silas is rejoicing in the opportunity and is busily preparing for the enterprise!

After much prayer and visible support from the local Church, we farewelled the pair, pleading for news of them whenever possible. The Church Council scanned the map which outlined the intended route:

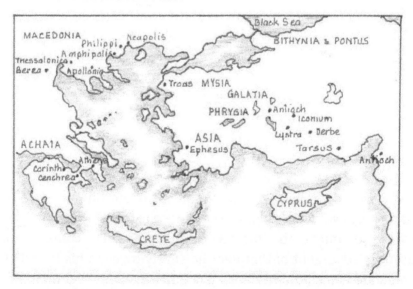

It is good to report here that it did not seem an inordinate amount of time before word was forthcoming to the effect that another young man by the name of Timothy had joined the team in Lystra. How good is that?! In the town where Paul had been stoned with almost mortal consequences, here was a young man—already a disciple—ready to face the rigours of joining forces with Paul and Silas. We think, from the report, that Timothy has the full blessing of his mother, a Jewess, though we could gather no information regarding his father who is a Greek.

One of the major aims of Paul's team is to share the all-important evidence—via the official document—that the Jerusalem Church is totally in favour of Gentiles being accepted as fully accredited Christians without the need to undergo the demands of Jewish Law. The actual letter is produced and the signatures appearing on the parchment give full credence to the decision reached in Jerusalem. The outcome is that the Communities of Faith throughout the region are gathering strength—spiritually and numerically—as new people were added daily to the Church.

The team is moving at the direction of the Holy Spirit and we are delighted to know that the Lord is caring for them in this way. In his communication with us who remain in Antioch, Paul has reported a remarkable happening where, one night, he had a vision of a Macedonian man standing before him. This man requested that Paul and his team go to Macedonia to help the people of that region. Paul recognised that he was being called of the Lord to move into Macedonia with his message and his manpower! He was to leave Asia!

Well, the three men—Paul, Silas and Timothy were being aided now by another eager participant: a doctor, no less. I am particularly pleased about that. Paul is not really all that robust physically though the muscle power of his spirit is magnificent! Paul appears to have a very positive attitude with regard to this young man Timothy. Certainly, the extra pair of hands will be of invaluable assistance to the worthy warrior!

The work is expanding in Antioch. Onesimus in his kitchen, Demetrius, the pedagogue–cum–youth worker, out in the field with his many followers, Maryam and her team—Eustace and Angela—working their fingers to the bone in the clinic, and the leadership team with our preaching and teaching responsibilities, are all seeing such good results for our labours. I have been noticing a change in Maryam, though. Her enthusiasm for the work has in no way abated. But Maryam is tired.

Onesimus mentioned the matter to me just two nights ago when Maryam sought her bed covers earlier than usual. 'Pastor Pa, I wish I could do more to ease her burdens but at home, she hustles me away when I attempt to take over the kitchen sink!' 'Let's be on the lookout, Onesimus. If some things can be done before her return from the clinic, we may be able to ease her burden somewhat. In the meantime, I will search out some extra help for her.'

As the leader in our Church, Ambrose is such an encourager. He endeavours to support every program as it takes its course. He has been a great help to me during the series on Prayer which has reached its climactic stages. I may have been the planner and the programmer but, as teacher, I—Manaen ben Baruch—have also learned much for I have sought the Lord's guidance. As I endeavoured to develop the themes based on the outlines, I have been enriched. Prayer is not merely a subject to be taught, it is an experience to be enjoyed, an avenue to be walked, a communion to be encountered.

Prayer is the difference between a desert and a garden! We talked about that thought one morning in class. It was quite moving to be intimately involved with the course members as they described their own desert experiences and how, through faith, the gentle showers of blessing fell upon them to bring relief from an arid journey into an enriching walk beside still waters—to quote the psalmist, always helpful—so that the soul is again restored to health!

I was beginning to consider how best Maryam could enjoy the summer break that was coming up fast. A month and then we could relax. The clinic would be wound down for clientele would engage themselves in the pleasantries of the summer sun. Onesimus would be well able to handle any emergency. As for me, I have reached the final section of our studies on Prayer—now well into "The Results of Prayer"—and we were happily recounting the many evidences where "Thankfulness" becomes the oft repeated response to the Lord's daily care of each individual life.

How wonderful it is to listen to the accounts of thankfulness for the miracles that people have encountered in their lives. And with what joy I recognise a thankfulness for just a kindly thought, the lifting of a burden by another, the wordless smile for a benefactor along the path of need. Our people have been learning the grace of thankfulness.

Next week we will be challenged by the final segment of the series, that of "Resolution—The resolve to place myself in God's will." I've said it often, I know, but I place myself in the "firing line" where an arrow may find its mark as I recognise how important it is that the teacher does not place himself—or herself, for that matter—above the situation of the student. The teacher who has ceased to learn is no longer a viable teacher for he can no longer relate to personal circumstance. Therefore, my personal challenge becomes: what of the future now?

What is the road ahead for me? For Manaen ben Baruch this must also include the welfare of my beloved *Mimi*, Maryam. I have given Maryam into the care of the Lord since the night of our marriage. I do not intend to change my attitude. Nor does the LORD require this of me. However, what does He now require of me, of us?

How timely are the challenges of the Lord?! One ought to be more ready, to wait now upon the doorstep of opportunity. Or—

conversely—to be prepared for an immensity of blessing only to find that doorway closing one's hopes away from sight. Well, the courier carrying Paul's letter addressed to me was a timely missive, to say the least of it. Upon opening the seal, I nearly dropped the document! It read:

Paul, your "Terrific Troubler"

Philippi

Eastern Macedonia

Late Spring.

To Manaen,

my reputable rabbinic reasoner,

Summer is approaching and I'd like to think that you are too! Seriously, Manaen, and Maryam, it is time for you to relax a while. For many summers you have given of yourselves to the ministry and, though you have stayed put, your energy has given itself to the very limits of endurance. I have watched you at your work. The both of you are missionaries in heart and hand.

It's not the ground one treads that marks one out for mission—it's the fervour in the hands and in the heart, the soul. So! Do what I did for that long time in Antioch while you, Maryam, ministered to those many welts upon my back and you, Manaen, as I accosted you with my diatribes. Also, to be serious again, you listened to my quandaries regarding Galatia. I must say that our discussions have worked out well.

Now, the purpose for this letter? It's an invitation to you both. Come to Philippi. There are some people I want you to meet. You'll be impressed and I do assure you that you will rejoice in the outcome of the enterprise. Besides, the sea voyage will be of benefit to you.

There is no time to waste. Decide now. No toing and froing of the mind. Say yes! Do come! You will receive blessing after blessing in Philippi. My courier must return on the tide so make up your mind!

Grace and peace to you both!

From Paul

(You are aware that I write in a large hand. I took to the pen myself to emphasise the import of this invite!) Please give my personal greetings to Onesimus. I am most impressed with that young man!

I all but fell over myself in the rush to reach Maryam with this amazing correspondence. Her reaction was to be expected, of course. There was no hint of excitement in her reaction but, then again, no evidence of negativity. Maryam just smiled at me and then all so slowly nodded her agreement with the invitation. Yes! We would go to Philippi!

In checking out the credentials of the city, we discovered that it was a Roman colony and was, indeed, the most prominent city of Eastern Macedonia. The city was named after Philip, the father of that Greek of highest accolade: Alexander the Great. It would have been so helpful if Onesimus could have journeyed with us but he was quite vehement in his rejection of the offer. I realised, of course, that the journey would have taken him nearer to his earlier life. Our "adopted son", however, sprang into the necessary packing and bagging of the essentials for the journey. He assured us of his diligence to take care of everything while we would be absent. We found that we could wholly trust him now.

We were able to take greater interest in our surroundings as we arrived at the sea port near Antioch. It seemed like an eon of time ago that Maryam and I, together with our travelling companion Nicolas, had reached these shores as refugees from all but certain death at the hands of our royal enemy, Herod, in Jerusalem. All fear was gone. The day was pleasantly warm with just a gentle sea breeze that would fill the sails of the Roman ship bound to carry us out into the great "Middle Sea".

The embarkation took place with little ado and we were escorted to our sleeping quarters. Thankfully, we discovered that there was adequate sleeping space. The baggage—which included some substantial provisions for Paul and his team— were secured and then we returned to the deck to view the receding shores of Syria.

Conditions continued to be most acceptable. A gentle rolling with the tide still allowed us some freedom in movement around the deck next morning. As we journeyed near to the north of Cyprus, our thoughts were drawn to Barnabas and his nephew, John Mark. How were they faring? We had had no word of them. But we could pray for them. And we did.

On the following day, we were awakened by a distinct change in the weather conditions. The ship was no longer at peace with its surroundings! Maryam remained in her bunk. I ventured to check the conditions up on deck. I wished I hadn't. A certain queasiness all but overcame me. I clung to the railing as I observed, quite hastily before returning to my bunk, that the sails were furled. The sailors were scurrying about securing the hatches, advising me to return to my quarters without delay. 'We will allow the ship to ride out the storm. Have no fear!' With this positive word, I went back to Maryam who, I discovered, had taken quite ill. I must confess that I felt very much like copying her ejections into the available basin! Sea sickness, I believe, is the term used generally for our malaise.

By the time we had reached Rhodes, the storm had abated and our ship and its cargo—human and otherwise—having received no major damage, were able to relax in the port before resuming the voyage to Ephesus—our next port of call. From thence, we travelled due north to Samothrace. The sailors informed us that they were always glad to see this port "approaching" as the ship sailed confidently into its calm and inviting waters. We stayed on board that night, ready for the hoisting of sails on the early morning high tide the following day.

We disembarked finally at Neapolis where we were met by a warmly welcoming man by the name of Damion. A thoroughly efficient helper, Damion soon had us on our way, travelling the short distance westward to Philippi. Maryam, substantially weakened by the sea voyage, and I were awaiting with great eagerness our reunion with Paul and Silas. And, of course, we would be meeting up with young Timothy as well.

It was a welcome not far short of a robust hugging that then greeted us as Paul rushed to us with arms outstretched. Then he clapped his hands. 'Come, there are people to meet!' By now, we were greatly anticipating the meeting of people alluded to in his letter of invitation. It wouldn't be long now.

Paul turned to a woman, whom I could best describe as stately, and beckoned her. Here was a person above the average at first glance at least and, as we came to know Lydia, our initial assessment was more than realised. At once, this gracious woman came to Maryam and with an unfeigned warmth assisted her to a comfortable seat then stayed with her as I was still engaged with the highly exuberant Paul.

I had hardly sufficient time to greet Silas when another young man, obviously a Greek scarcely out of his teens, I thought, was presented. His name was Timothy! My first reaction was most positive, I could see by his physique and confident stance, why Paul was delighted to include him in the team.

Following a very welcome meal, Paul drew attention to a man of athletic build and confident demeanour who was approaching. His face exuded "welcome"! Paul reminded me that there were people here that he wanted me to meet. One, I had already been able to greet—Lydia, who was even now ministering to the quite frail Maryam. 'Manaen, this is a good friend to me: Doctor Luke!' The usual comments were exchanged: 'Pleased to meet you...' 'I've heard much about you' and such like. Then some serious conversations took place.

Paul was aware that Maryam needed medical attention and the invitation had been sent especially for her benefit. The doctor placed Maryam under observation, discussed her symptoms at length and delivered his findings to both man and wife together. Maryam was in need of a prolonged rest cure. Her strength needed to be rebuilt. He advised that a pleasant stay in Philippi under the watchful eye of Lydia would achieve the best results. We were keen to follow doctor's orders! And Paul was also aware that I was searching for a medical man to participate in my shared project with the Apostle John to commence a Second Edition, as it were, of the Holy Scriptures. We were intent on producing a New Testament and the beginnings of its scripting was already taking the first tentative steps.

Paul's two-pronged invitation was no off-the-cuff idea, no decision born of a whim! Here possibly, is the man who could bring another contribution to the project by focussing on the miraculous healings wrought by the Rabbi from Galilee—the Man who would bring about the salvation of the world.

Doctor Luke and I struck a harmonious chord that has not abated in the time since we first shook hands on a deal that would help to change the world. Dr Luke's pen and parchment would describe, in particular, Jesus—the Man. In accepting the request, Luke pointed out that he would need to rely on the firsthand evidence of people who knew Jesus and who could produce eye-witness accounts of major incidents in His ministry.

How happy I was to provide a beginning for Luke's document by describing the Bethlehem scenes where angels sang and donkeys brayed. He was surprised to discover that it was my own father who was the shepherd that led his companions into the stable on the night of Jesus' birth. I could tell of a held hand, of a presentation of precious gifts to that little *kebaa–baa–baas* boy by strangers—magi, travellers from far to the east to pay homage to "The King born to be Man." Luke picked up his pen at that!

The rapport established between Dr Luke and myself kept us in converse concerning the project. His enthusiasm for the task saw no bounds. One morning, Luke brought a new humility to me packaged up in his surprisingly moving comment that it was time for me to take on a Greek appellation to my name.

I looked at this dauntless man with affection and inquired, with some humour, what the nature of such an appendage would be. Without pause, Luke replied, 'I would like to name you, just between ourselves, *"Theophilus".'* '"Theophilus"—the friend of

God?' 'Yes, Manaen, I see that affinity well portrayed in your life. You are an inspiration to me and I will be honoured to participate in your project. I can't wait to meet with the Apostles John, Peter and others who will assist me in the task. I will send my sealed writings addressed to *"Theophilus"* in acknowledgement of the honour you have placed in my hands!' What could I say to that? A firm grip of Luke's skilful hand perhaps carried my response in the best possible way. But I was humbled by this momentous encounter.

Paul took his leave of us, needing to press on into new territory. Dr Luke was to accompany him as had been the case since that vision in which Paul received his "marching orders" to enter into Macedonian territory. Maryam and I remained in Philippi with Lydia who continued to oversight my wife's recovery. It was so gratifying to see Maryam grow strong once more. I took note of the fact that the two women had become firm friends. This friendship would solidify and deepen as both faced the future that stretched out before them.

We fell into an easy relationship as our family stories were exchanged. Lydia, of course, was amazed at Maryam's personal history. She was advised to keep Maryam's royal background a secret for it would be inappropriate to spread it abroad—for more than one reason!

In turn, how delighted we were to hear Lydia's account of her introduction to Christianity. Lydia had already been a person who worshipped God and a visit to the local riverside brought her into contact with Paul who had come to that location in order to be refreshed. He took the opportunity to proclaim the Good News about Jesus Christ. Lydia described how the Lord had opened her heart to receive the Gospel and the rest is history!

Lydia, it was discovered, is a woman of some wealth as she is a trader in cloth coloured in a rare purple dye harvested from a shell fish of that region. Maryam explained that even the wife of Herod gained her gorgeous gowns via this highly sought-after cloth!

Lydia also informed us of the surprising fact that Paul and Silas had been imprisoned in Philippi as an outcome of the ceaseless rantings of a sorceress. Paul had, finally, taken control. He commanded that the evil spirit come away from the woman. At once her prattling ceased but her slave-owners were less than impressed. Their ready means of gathering coinage for their coffers also ceased! They dragged Paul and Silas into the marketplace, brought them before the city magistrates and accused the two of being Jews who were causing an uproar.

Paul and Silas were stripped, then flogged and thrown into prison. The jailer was given specific instructions to guard them closely—there was no telling what they might do! 'Manaen, Maryam, would you believe it? There they were, held by chains, in agony from the flogging but singing duets in praise of God! About midnight, there was a severe earthquake. The prison shook! The doors flew open. The chains fell off—every prisoner, free!

Lydia continued: 'The jailer awoke. He looked at the devasting results of the quake and was about to kill himself—his life for every prisoner who had, no doubt escaped! Paul took things in hand. "Stop! Don't harm yourself. We are all here— every man of us!" "What, it can't be so," the jailer screamed. "See for yourself. Here we are: free but remaining here. We had to think of you!" 'Friends, the jailer ran for a lantern, took stock of the situation, fell to his knees and pleaded, "Sirs, what must I do to be saved?" He then heard those precious words: "Believe in the Lord Jesus Christ and you will be saved, your family too."

'The jailer and his wife ministered to Paul and Silas, bathing their wounds and providing a meal for them. He and his family acknowledged faith in Christ and were received into the Community of Faith with prayers of thanksgiving and consecration.

'Next morning the magistrates sought to take control of the situation. They sent officials to order the release of Paul and Silas. The jailer's pleasure was a sight to behold as he relayed the edict of the court to the men. "You are released. You are free to leave. Go in peace!"

'Paul, however, was not to be deterred from placing a firm fist on the situation. He addressed himself to the officials. "We were beaten mercilessly without a trial. This happened even though both of us are Roman citizens! We were thrown into prison. Now the magistrates want to wash their hands of the whole debacle by having us escorted from the city? We refuse to exit without due recognition of the circumstances. Let the magistrates come themselves to escort us out!"

'The officials went back to the magistrates with this amazing missive. The magistrates were all but prostrate! "Roman citizens? These men are Roman citizens? We will come at once. Let there be no further disturbance. We cannot have the Roman hierarchy breathing down our necks. Of course, we will escort them from the prison and request that they leave the city as soon as possible." 'Well, friends, both men came to my home where we were able to arrange a meeting with the brethren before Paul and Silas left us. We were pleased with their unscheduled return to await your arrival in Philippi.'

As we whiled away those lazy summer months, word would reach the Community of Faith at Philippi of the progress of Paul's mission that was now well into the thick of all the prior planning. Word from Thessalonica—along the Egnatian Way—confirmed that Paul had gone initially to the well-established Jewish community there. He visited the synagogue. Many people—both Jews and Greeks—responded by joining the Community of Faith.

Trouble had erupted as indignant Jews caused a clamour that reached through the whole area. A believer by the name of Jason was sheltering the team. But when the frenzied mob reached his dwelling, the missionaries could not be found.

In order to appease their anger, the mob dragged Jason and others from his home and presented them to the city officials with the accusation: 'These men are causing trouble all over the world, now they have come here and Jason is welcoming them! They are all asserting that someone named Jesus is the King, not Caesar!' Jason was duly admonished but released. At night-fall, the brethren secreted Paul and his associates out of the city.

Berea was next on Paul's agenda. It was good to receive a message to the effect that the Jews of this area were much more inclined to listen to the Gospel. Many were saved—including leading citizens—and it was only when certain agitators from Thessalonica arrived that matters became perilous. It was decided that Silas and Timothy would remain in Berea but that Paul should move on. He headed for Athens.

Athens proved to be a time of great distress to Paul for the whole city was overrun with idols—here and there, everywhere—idols of every style: wooden, stone, pottery, every possible commodity. Then he went to the Areopagus on Mars Hill dedicated to the god of thunder and war—*Ares*: in Roman parlance, *Mars*.

Paul's later report filled us with awe. This god-filled, Godless, city had given space to an unknown god. This was, in fact, the title appended in a most unusual form: *To the Unknown God*. What an opportunity presented itself to Paul.

We have an account of what he declared to the gathered crowd: 'I, Paul of Tarsus, am a visitor to your city. I am impressed by the many objects of worship I see before me. I am therefore aware that you are a very religious people. I have found one such shrine dedicated *To the Unknown God*. I am pleased to be able to declare before you all that the One whom you so devotedly worship without knowing His Name, I am able to introduce to you!'

One can only imagine the effect this announcement had upon the listeners. They must all have been agog in response to

Paul's assertion. He continued, we understand, with this disclosure: "The God I serve is the Creator of the universe! He does not exist in temples made with human hands though He is not far from any one of us: it is in Him that we live and move and have our being. As His children, we should not be trying to mould Him into shapes that human hands can erect with gold and silver or any kind of stone. Before we became aware of who God is, He overlooked our ignorant ways. But things have changed!

"I speak to you all for there is a need to change our ways, give due reverence to the Eternal God for He has now set in place a means by which what is wrong in this world can be made right. God has given His Son, Jesus—the *Christos*—to the world so that all may live by faith in Him. The actual proof that this is the truth is that this same Jesus was crucified on a hill just by the city of Jerusalem. What seals the giving of God is that His Son was raised from the dead on the third day following His death. He is now ascended to Heaven. His own Holy Spirit is with us now to grant us strength to live a holy life!"

Many in the crowd, we hear, laughed Paul to scorn but some listened carefully and requested that Paul give them further time to hear his message. One of the members of the Areopagus— Dionysius by name—was one of the few who took Paul's words to heart and became a follower of the Lord. Paul then moved on to Corinth.

The days were closing in. Soon autumn would be showing its colours to the world and requesting an extra cloak to stave off the cooler climate. Because the weather was presenting itself, however, in its most placid "apparel", Maryam and I decided that we should take an early opportunity to return to Antioch. It was quite an emotional farewell.

•••••••••••••••••

17. A WHITE STONE

Our friends at Antioch were elated at our return. Onesimus glowed with pleasure as we opened the door to our home. We were glad that there was time to add to the stew he was boiling up for his evening meal! The house was in excellent order—a tribute to our "adopted son". After we retired to our own room, Maryam broached the subject of the current status of Onesimus. 'Is it not time that we…?' 'Maryam, you are ready to receive him as your son?' 'Oh, yes, Manaen. He will never replace David in our hearts but he can stand beside him!' 'Maryam, beloved, we can rejoice in "family" again. I must confess that I have looked upon Onesimus as a son for some considerable time. He has burrowed his way into my life.' 'And also, mine. Let's tell him at breakfast.'

What a morning it proved to be. Onesimus almost choked on his buttered bun. A timely thump on the back brought him back to a better state of decorum! 'Pastor Pa, Mother Emi, it is your desire? That I should be your son? I can never remember being a son. I wonder if I can come up to the mark required of me?' 'Son! You are already there!' It was hug time. 'This morning, we will go to the city authorities to gain the necessary papers to seal our new relationship. I think we need the support of Ambrose as he is well respected in the city. He can stand guarantor of the application.'

Things did not run smoothly as we fronted up to the city officials. 'Who are your natural parents?' 'I have never known my parents. I am an orphan.' 'Where is your home?' 'I came away from home too early to remember. I lived on the streets and alleyways until going into service as a cook. I lost my way. My new parents found me, took me into their home. They have sheltered me, cared for me, guided me.' 'Be that as it may, we require the official documentation of your true identity.'

Only then did Onesimus begin to wilt. Ambrose saved the day. 'Sirs, I will vouch for this young man. He saved a person's life who all but died from snake bite. He serves with distinction as the chief cook in the Church. He now assists the "Serving Seven" who are dedicated to the alleviation of poverty in this city. Manaen is our leading teacher and his wife, Maryam, gives valued service in the clinic. Sirs, I believe these factors outweigh the lesser requirement of a piece of parchment that could verify the true identity of this worthy applicant and his wonderful guardians. Please, allow them to become this man's parents.' The speech was enough. A document was prepared, signed, sealed, and delivered! Onesimus held in his hand the official approval of his new status: Onesimus "son of Pastor Pa and Mother Emi"!

It was hardly a day for relaxing. It was a day for rejoicing and we were well into this happy festivity when Onesimus staggered me by his request for a white stone. 'A white stone, Son? I savoured the new title but asked again, 'A white stone? Go to the seaside, down any alleyway. You can easily find a white stone.' With that charming smile of his, Onesimus set me straight. 'That's not the kind of white stone I mean Pastor... oops, Papa, I think.' His happy chuckle then led into a serious discourse.

'There is a revered custom where, if a son is to be absent, or father absent from the son, a white stone is prepared on which is written a secret name known only to the parent and the son. Then, the stone is split in two. The father keeps one half and the other is given to the son. If ever there is any question regarding identity, either may produce his half of the stone. This is placed together with the other half so that the secret name is made plain for all to see. Because the two pieces fit together, it provides the proof of identity.' 'Onesimus, our son! What a magnificent custom. Please secure a white stone for us to prepare as our identity stone! We will determine the secret name then ask a stone mason for help. Oh, and by the way, have you thought of any special name that you would like to have inscribed on our stone?' 'Definitely Dad—ha ha—I have it already in mind. I do hope you can agree with it.' Onesimus took a piece of parchment and sketched an outline of a stone and, as he commenced writing his name, he made a comment that surprised both his mother and me. 'Papa, as my name could be spelt *Onesimos*, I think it will be alright to just change one more letter and we will have our secret name.' (For Biblical proof, see Revelation 2:12-17).

We watched in keen anticipation as our newly designated son proceeded to scrawl the name "One-Simon". 'The stone can be split before the "s". 'There we have it, Papa: ONE and SIMON. Simon means a stone, does it not? I want to be as solid as a rock for you and for your Lord! You can receive the half marked "ONE"—standing for *protos* for you are first and foremost in my life, and I will be "SIMON": "*rock*"-solid in my faithfulness to you and Mother Emi.' This was the icing on the cake, the settlement of the new ties that bound us in the cords of love and mutual respect. I loved the thought of being the *protos* for Onesimus!

The white stone, having been secured and the secret chosen name scratched upon its surface, there was added a well-defined and deep underscoring by my own hand. Onesimus and I made our way to a stone mason who nodded his agreement of the enterprise. Obviously there had been previous requests of a similar nature. The splitting of the stone was exact and, as we viewed the effect, we realised that there was another message on the stone:

Certainly, I rejoiced. I think that Onesimus did also! Maryam sealed the venture with a kiss for us both—near the cross!

Oh yes, it took time for everything to return to any sense of normality. I would need to commence my planning for the winter term of Biblical Studies at the Church. I was greatly exercised in my mind as to what would be of best benefit to the Christians at Antioch. Much prayer was needed for the enterprise and I began to focus on what the Lord would have me open up to our participants.

Meanwhile, word had reached us that Paul had moved on to Corinth. A later report that arrived by courier, made us aware of the recent happenings. It was here that Paul met Aquila—a Jew—who, with his wife had been hounded out of Rome as a result of an edict by Caesar Claudius.

This couple were tentmakers—as was Paul—so he worked together with them for some time, raising much-needed funds. Each Sabbath, he would speak in the local synagogue with excellent results until the inevitable "visitation" of disgruntled Jews who took exception to the content of Paul's preaching. That worthy man dusted off his cloak in front of them and declared, 'Your blood be on your own heads! I turn from you to the Gentiles who have the sensibility to listen to truth without rancour!' Surprisingly, it was Crispus, the ruler of that synagogue, who avowed his faith in the Good News of the Gospel and he and his entire household were baptised.

Paul was comforted by a vision where, in a direct conversation with the Lord, he was encouraged to continue speaking without fear.

Be assured, there are many people in this city who believe in Me.

While Gallio was proconsul in the area, Paul was hauled before the court and accused of issuing propaganda that was against Jewish Law. The proconsul delivered his determination: he was not responsible for Jewish arguments. 'Settle the matter yourselves,' he retorted carelessly. Then a fury swept over the antagonistic Jews, resulting in the thrashing of Sosthenes for not arguing their case more effectively. We are of the opinion that this man—a ruler of the synagogue—was a believer at heart. Perhaps he may come to actually support Paul.

It was some considerable time before we became aware that Paul was moving on to Ephesus in the good company of Priscilla and her husband, Aquilla—strange, the order of those names. Perhaps it indicates that Priscilla is a woman of some considerable note. *En route* to Ephesus, while at Cenchrea, Paul had his hair cut off to indicate that he had taken a vow. Surely the Jews would recognise his intent and respect the man for his devout attitude to the Lord!

The last word was that Paul and his friends had reached Ephesus—a thriving centre of commerce and the provincial capital—where, as was his practice, he made his way to the synagogue in the hope of a warm and ready response to the Gospel message. It was discovered that, though the citizens knew of Jesus, they had never heard of the Holy Spirit. They relied on the baptism of John the Baptist. Paul opened their minds and hearts to the Good News. Many responded in faith and there was a mighty outpouring of the Spirit among them.

The results of Paul's ministry were extraordinary and he remained among this new and thriving Church for a great length of time. When, finally, it became imperative for him to depart, the citizens pleaded for Paul to remain with them as they needed to hear more of this amazing Gospel he was preaching. Paul explained that he was obligated to return to Antioch via Caesarea though he did promise to come again if at all possible. This news means that we can expect him quite soon.

How good it will be to have Paul describe to me the nature of his ministry in Ephesus. I longed, also, to hear more of the preaching of an Alexandrian by the name of Apollos who was a dynamic God-fearer. In his forthright preaching, Apollos spoke often of Jesus but he was unfamiliar with much of the Gospel. He espoused the ministry of John the Baptist. Priscilla and Aquilla set him right. Filled with the Holy Spirit, Apollos determined to go to Achaia with the Gospel and the Church members supported him, providing him with letters of endorsement and requesting that he be welcomed wholeheartedly. Apollos was "well worth his salt" for he was an avid preacher, proclaiming the Gospel publicly and engaging in vigorous debate. It was from the Holy Scripture, I am informed, that Apollos was able to emphasise that Jesus is the Christ, promised from early ages! I will keep this in mind.

In the meantime, Paul and a growing number of assistants, was travelling steadily through Macedonia and Greece, visiting those who had come to faith during his previous missionary journeys. There is an amazing account of how Paul was able—in the power of the Holy Spirit—to restore a young man, by the name of Eutychus, to life after he had fallen from a high window on to the street below.

It looks very much like the Church at Antioch will have to

forego its "welcome home" to Paul. The most recent communication we have received indicates that he is intent on reaching Jerusalem by the Festival of Pentecost. Perhaps he may make his way back to us after his journey to Jerusalem. We hear that he is in Ephesus to bid farewell to his beloved "family" there. The final word on that farewell was of a gathering bathed in tears. All realised that they may not meet with Paul again this side of Heaven.

One day, a courier brought a message to me from Philip the Evangelist—the man who all those years ago had brought an Ethiopian through to faith in Christ, one of the very first conversions of a Gentile—who was currently hosting Paul. He informs me that a man by the name of Agabus had, with the aid of a belt—taken from Paul—which he bound about himself like that of a prisoner, then prophesied that the owner of the belt would soon find himself in a similar circumstance. Paul was about to be handed over to the Roman authorities! Paul was not deterred but continued on his way.

Paul's re-entry into Jerusalem was noised abroad and the Jewish authorities, we hear, took it upon themselves to be rid of this troublesome antagonist. There had, however, been the warmest of welcomes from James and the brethren. Paul devised a plan to indicate his obedience, and those of his travelling companions, to the best principles of The Law. It was not good enough as some Jews of the Diaspora—dispersed Jews—espied him in the Temple and gave vent to their feelings. Paul was pronounced a traitor to the Hebrew cause! The city went into a crazed uproar. Paul was seized with the intent to assassinate him. The Roman commander got wind of the rabble-rousing tumult in the city and promptly went with troops to quell the riot.

Paul, it is reported, asked permission to speak to the crowd after assuring the commander that he was, indeed, a Jew— certainly not the Egyptian terrorist as was supposed. Then, the commander agreed. Paul spoke his piece. He spoke in Aramaic. That surprised his accusers! Perhaps there was something in what he was preaching after all! Paul presented his personal witness of his complete turn-around from terrorist to apostle. Things were going well until he explained the reason for his decision to take the Gospel to the Gentile world. That was it. With that one sentence he had sealed his own fate! 'Down with him! Traitor!'

Paul was held in the Roman garrison overnight. A plot to kill the apostle was overheard by Paul's nephew and the Roman guard was alerted. The lad was taken to the commander who cautioned him to tell no one of this report. He took charge of the situation, ordering a troop of two hundred men to escort Paul to Caesarea. He must be taken to Governor Felix. A letter was detached via the centurion in charge which gave explanation regarding Paul and the reason for his detainment. The Roman guard in Jerusalem had, in fact, saved Paul's life.

The report was absorbed and a decision was made to keep Paul in detention at Herod's Caesarean Palace. Maryam and I thought of going to plead his cause though we gravely doubted that Herod would be prone to listen to his half-sister and brother-in-law—absconders from his "protective care" in the Jerusalem residence.

Paul gave due deference to the local governor in his statement of defence. The man was well aware of the teachings of the Christian sect and had acknowledged that Paul should be treated with respect. He was not inclined to make a hasty decision however, deciding to await the arrival of Felix. That august personage arrived some long time later and listened to the prisoner until things became quite delicate with regard to Paul's obvious faith in Jesus, reputed to be the Christ. 'That's enough for today. I will give consideration to your defence and engage in a further hearing at a later date.' (Felix was a man, it was whispered, who was keen to elicit a sizeable bribe in order to secure a man's freedom). Felix took his time and it was such a long time, stretching out to about two years! Finally, Felix was relieved of his post and Porcius Festus was appointed in his place. To please his Jewish agitators, Felix had left Paul biding his time in prison.

As matters deteriorated during that two-year period, Onesimus came to me one evening with an unprecedented request. 'Papa, could you possibly agree to me going to Caesarea to be of assistance to the Apostle Paul? He is in much need of the kind of attention that I can best give him. In my previous life, I attended to all the personal needs of my owner. I want to be of help to Paul. What do you say?' I called Maryam to our side and reiterated our new son's request.

Maryam showed no distress at the request but did point out that the task ahead of him was fraught with danger. We spoke of the negative aspects but then, also, the positives and—at the end of our deliberations—it was agreed that Onesimus should do as he requested. He was prepared for perhaps the inevitability of dire circumstance.

The young man put his hand into his belt pouch and lifted his piece of our white stone. In turn, I went to my own belt pouch and pulled out the other half. We placed the pieces together, saw again the secret name and also the sign—that of the cross, formed by the broken stone. It was enough. Faith would see him, and us, through this inevitable parting. Would we ever know the joy of seeing our new son again? We were doubtful and a certain sadness crept over us.

Following a rather emotional farewell by the Community of Faith in Antioch, particularly that of Demetrius and Astrid—whose life Onesimus had saved—Onesimus went, with our blessing, down to the port from whence he set sail for Caesarea. Paul was pathetically pleased, I know, to see this young man so intent on attending to his every need.

It was discovered that Dr Luke had remained with Paul and he was currently engaged in interviewing a number of the eye-witnesses to the earthly life of Jesus. Luke's parchments are filling up with wonderful episodes that will, certainly, be described in graphic detail in the future *New* Testament.

18. INNER COMPASS POINTS

Life must go on. News of Onesimus, and Paul, was scarce. I had been struggling for some time to weave together a study course for the winter term. The first class was to commence the following week. Lord, help me! The theme will need to be announced during the Worship Service on the Lord's Day. Again, 'Lord, help me!' I am prone to recall the many conversations I have enjoyed with Paul. I remember how frequently he would speak of the *IN*-look that gives rise to one's *OUT*-look on life. I suddenly realise that I'm on to something here. 'Thanks, Lord!' I will follow Paul's lead. How thoroughly enlightening! The "Terror from Tarsus" has evolved into my "Trusted Teacher"! My faithful writing kit will record the all-important outline of the Winter Theme:

THE *IN*-LOOK ON LIFE

It should be noted that most of these topics are the product of Paul's insights. Perhaps all students will one day find his teaching on this theme in the letters that he had sent via one of his faithful couriers to the Church in Corinth. The course began to take shape, largely from Paul's insights:

ON WHOM DO YOU RELY?

1 The Lord will reveal His will for our lives
2 The Holy Spirit Guide is received as a free gift through faith

3 Spoken words are an expression of spiritual truth
4   The Spirit aids discernment between good and evil
5 Right judgement is the result of trust
6 Human judgement is inferior to spiritual insight
7 We are gifted with insight from Christ.

WHERE IS YOUR GIFTING?

1	WISDOM	The ability to apply knowledge
2	KNOWLEDGE	Intellect of high quality
3	FAITH	In the "night" as well as the "day"
4	HEALING	Prayerful, believing treatment of the frail
5	MIRACLES	Outstanding achievement beyond norm
6	DISCERNMENT	Between good and evil
7	PROPHECY	Inspiration proclaimed

WHAT IS YOUR ATTITUDE?

1 DIVERSITY in HUMANITY Illustrated by human body
2 SELF: I'm the foot   I'm not the hand: I don't belong
              I'm the ear   I'm not the eye: I don't belong
3 EVERYONE: THE EYE?   How could we hear?
    EVERYONE AN EAR?   How could we detect aromas?
4 THE EYE CAN'T SAY: You're the ear: I don't need you
5 ALL: TREATED EQUALLY None more "equal" than others
6 IF ONE SUFFERS: All should be attentive, helpful
    IF ONE IS HONOURED   All should be rejoicing
7 GOD'S APPOINTMENT: Prophets, Teachers, Healers, Helpers...
                                    (Not everyone has the same Calling)

WHAT IS YOUR NATURE?

Are you the most talented? Without LOVE =
                            a clanging cymbal.
Are you a prophet who knows life's mysteries? No LOVE =
                            it means nothing.
Do you possess great Faith? Without LOVE =
                            it means nothing!
Are you the most generous of all? Without LOVE =
                            you will gain nothing!

THE ATTITUDES OF LOVE:

1 PATIENCE: Ability to bear with adversity
2 KINDNESS: The practical outcome of Love
3 NO ENVY, BOASTING, PRIDE: These lead to rudeness, selfishness
4 NOT EASILY PROVOKED: Slow to anger, No scoring of wrongs
5 NO DELIGHT IN EVIL: Rejects ungodliness
6 REJOICES IN THE TRUTH: Recognises and applauds veracity
7 PROTECTS–TRUSTS–HOPES–PERSEVERES: Love never fails!

WHAT IS THE STRENGTH OF YOUR FAITH?

1 EVERYTHING COMES TO ITS FINAL CLIMAX: We will meet God
2 ALL THINGS WILL BE PERFECTED: Everything is in God's hands
3 THE IMPERFECT WILL DISAPPEAR: Human frailty gone
4 WE DEVELOP BEYOND UNUSED BRAIN OF A BABY: Mind power
5 TODAY WE SEE BUT DIMLY THROUGH GLASS: Physical limitations
6 ONE DAY WE WILL SEE FACE TO FACE: Know as we are known
7 THREE THINGS STAND THE TEST: Faith, Hope, Love—
                                Greatest of these: LOVE!

WHY DO YOU HOPE?
The Fulfilment of Life's Journey

1   If no resurrection: the Christian Gospel is futile
2   By one man came death   By One Man comes Life
3   How will we be raised?   Look at a seed!
4   Sow: the perishable   Weak—Natural
      Raised: imperishable   Power—Spiritual
5   Adam: dust   2nd Adam: Life-giving Spirit
                                * We bear Adam's likeness
                                * We *will* bear the Lord's likeness
6 We shall be changed: In a momentous blink of an eye
7 The mortal will be re-clothed: we will put on immortality

Death is swallowed up in victory
Death will not be victorious. The sting of death has gone
The sting was sin. The power of sin was The Law
Thank God, we will gain the victory!

158

The final list is a reflection of the Apostle John's projected thoughts on Apocalyptic events. He will not mind this early airing of his revelations that concern the End Times: No doubt he will structure his final work on the powerful figure 7. He has certainly guided me in these matters. Special emphasis will be given to John's "eye-openers":

WHAT DO YOU EXPECT IN THE ETERNAL DAWN?
This is what Heaven will be like

1   AN OPEN DOOR INTO ETERNAL SPLENDOUR
    Transcendence of time and space: the limited will become limitless

2   SEE JESUS FACE TO FACE
    Receive His welcome smile as you enter your prepared Home

3   GAIN ETERNAL LIFE
    We HAVE eternal life. In Heaven it is consummated
    There will be no sickness, suffering, death

4   THE MEETING WITH LOVED ONES
    Reunion with family, friends, who have gone on before us

5   RECOGNITION OF THE MARTYRS
    Observe their honoured place in the Avenues of Heaven

6   RECOGNITION OF BIBLICAL CHARACTERS
    Abraham, David, Isaiah... Recognition comes through familiarity

7   FIND YOUR NAME IN THE BOOK OF LIFE
    A place is reserved for all: all who believe in Christ shall not perish!

....

I patted my writing kit affectionately, well pleased now with the reflections given to me by these two great rabbis. Their missionary endeavours have taken them into far distant places. They have torn down the fences of bigotry, smashed down the walls of hatred, ignorance and indifference. Their voices, no doubt, will echo down the generations, ages and empires to come. Their work will not be in vain. And I intend to continue to do all in my power to support them and assist in the proclamation of the Gospel even if it is restricted to the classroom at the meeting hall in Antioch. This is where the Lord has appointed me to be His ambassador... But I do hope for some word of Onesimus, with his "One–Simon", in the not-too-distant future.

A Manaen teaching course would not be complete without the opening up of my writing kit to express the theme in Manaen ways! I go to my kit and find, before the end of the day, that a poem-cum-hymn has emerged. As I had set myself to the task, some thoughts that I had gathered during a worship service when Maryam and I were recuperating at Philippi, came to mind. There were the obvious echoes of the preaching of Paul in what has emerged:

THE EXAMPLE OF JESUS
(Tune: *Benediction* L.M.)

Here is the great encouragement
To be united now with Christ:
This is the comfort of His love,
The fellowship of lives so blessed.

So that all joy should be complete,
Unite your mind with Jesus' goal;
Reflect His own exampled love,
Be one in purpose: pure and whole.

Have no ambition trained on self,
No vain conceit, no false renown.
Consider others more the blessed;
Look on their interests, not your own.

CROSS ROADS

Oh, let your attitude be like
The attitude of Christ, our Lord;
In nature, He's unique with God,
He came to us to prove His Word.

He knew the path of servanthood,
He came to be like us so that
We all could be like unto Him;
He went to Calvary for that!

Therefore, He is exalted now
That, at His name, His holy Name,
We all should bow and praise the Lord,
Confessing His transcendent fame.

Our glorious hope is not confined:
From Christ, our Lord, we will not part;
We lift our song to highest Heaven,
It is our Home, Goal of the heart!

....

There is always a sense of relief when all the preparatory work has been completed. One can then be more confident that all will be well as our many students arrived for those early morning sessions on the Lord's Day. It has become a natural progression from the classroom to the sanctuary in the meeting hall for combined worship—everyone, from the children to the oldest of the elders—would gather here to worship as a "family". Often, we would find a sanctuary in the midst of our classroom discussions and debates, our sharing and our caring!

The weeks went by and I must confess that, at times, there were doubts mingled with the certainties. It's as things ought to be, I have maintained, for faith is born out of conquered doubts and, the greater the vanquished doubt, the greater will be the strength of faith! Our people continue to grow spiritually, to trust, to act in accordance with the will of the Lord. Our people are relying on the power of the Holy Spirit to ensure their continued allegiance and participation in the life and witness of the Community of Faith. Here are a people well named: they are Christians not just because of their alignment with the Church but because they emulate the character and the presence of Christ's Spirit in both their word and their witness.

The Apostle John has returned. It is always a blessing to the mind and soul to see his shining face as he enters once more into our company.

Joy! Oh, joy! He speaks his need to share some quality time with me. 'First, John, you are to relax. Recuperate! The thing is, Onesimus is no longer with us.' I explained his hasty departure and John was duly impressed. 'You could occupy his room in our home. What do you say? Maryam and her helpers are well versed in sparking up the ailing muscles of a missionary!' John agreed without hesitation. I was glad to see his pleasure at the invitation.

John settled in with us and, when he had gathered some restorative input from the Manaen *ben* Baruch household, he would sit at length to chat with me over the matters that were exercising his mind.

'Tell me about your itinerary—your circuit—John. Which are the churches given into your oversight and responsibility?' He pulled out some parchment on which was sketched the route by which he traversed the country associated with the seven churches in his care. We studied the document together, John pointing to the terrain where a hike was no easy endeavour. I am amazed at the man's resilience. My good friend became quite animated, though at times he would find it difficult to suppress some evident levels of anxiety.

'What is the... I'm looking for a word... What is the character of these centres, John? The "snow" in my hair will confirm that I would find it difficult to trek through those domains but my interest does not abate.' John took a deep breath and reminded me of our prior discussion but realised the need to speak to a broader canvas now. He pointed, first, to the great city of **Ephesus**.

'This is the most important city of Western Asia Minor. The great river—Cayster—empties into the Aegean Sea, nearby. It holds, therefore, a strategic position as a major trade route between east and west. The city boasts about the glory of its great idol: Diana—that is, Artemis—though it must be said that Paul's ministry in the city had been the means of turning many to faith in my Friend and all Christians: Jesus, the Christ. Since Paul's departure there have been a number of problems emerging. Oh, they work hard, they take their stand against wickedness. Certainly, they have not grown weary but my fear is that they serve the Lord from the standpoint of duty rather than a heartfelt love. There are definite anomalies that I must strive to correct. They need to reassess their attitudes. I desire that they will be judged able to enter into Paradise.'

John then pointed to a centre named **Smyrna**. It was an area about which I knew very little although it was rumoured that the Church in that city was facing immense difficulty. John confirmed this. He indicated that the believers throughout that region were suffering greatly, severely persecuted and also poverty stricken. John's description pointed to a group he described as counterfeit Jews—Jews by name but not nature! 'Manaen, Smyra is a beautiful Asian city but the population is largely enamoured of Rome! The believers have nothing in their pockets but, in their hearts, they are rich beyond measure! I hold grave fears for them as I see signs that they will be hounded even to death. They may well die as martyrs but they will be spared eternal death!'

'What of **Pergamum**?' 'The city has been built on a high cone-shaped hill and so flaunts itself as "The Citadel"! Pergamum's problem is that it also flaunts its wickedness. The believers however, endeavour to remain true to their Christian principles but are tempted at times. For example, they idolise the things that captivate their physical desires and it becomes difficult for the hungry to resist forbidden foods. I have had need also to counsel our people with regard to chaste behaviour. They have a need to seal their relationship with the Lord. I have to emphasise that "the Bread of Life" will nourish their souls.

'Manaen, the Christian Community at **Thyatira** can hardly be called "Christian" for most would need to be labelled "counterfeit Christians"!

Seleucus founded this city as a military outpost. It has grown in status and is now a major trading hub. Many guilds have their centres there. I believe you know Lydia very well, having met her in Philippi. Lydia, however, is from Thyatira and also sells her purple cloth in this city. I am trying regularly to encourage the local Christians not to engage in the evil practices so prevalent in the area. I endeavour to make the point that, if a Church is ailing, it has caught the ills that attack the heart and mind. The evil in their midst must be smashed just like cracked pottery. How many times must I counsel them to hold on to their faith?!

'Let's move on. My well-worn route takes me on to **Sardis**. At first glance, what could be better than the Church at Sardis?

Looks can be deceiving, Manaen. The faith of these people has a superficiality about it that grieves my heart. Everything appears to be a centre of vibrant Christianity but, underneath, this Church is sterile. There is no life—no vibrant faith! They live in the lap of luxury and are content with a life of ease—they laze about while the people perish! On my last visit, I admonished the group as a whole to gather up some fortitude, to recognise their lack. Yet, thank the Lord, there are some at least who have stayed clear of the tainted life of most Sardinians, living without smut ruining their inner and outer "garment" of righteousness—they have remained holy and have proved their worth. I'm convinced that their names will be written in the Book of Life.

'Now, here's a centre that lives up to its title! **Philadelphia**: *philia*! I love my visits to "The Friendly City". Theirs is an open door: they preach the Gospel in such a welcoming way that, currently, there is a revival and people are being won to the Lord daily! There is both numeric and spiritual growth. What a good combination! They keep the Faith. They know how to endure hardship and this results in enormous spiritual strength. Manaen, the way ahead for the Church at Philadelphia will present many challenges as the clouds of political unrest are hovering over the horizon. But that Community of Faith has the name of Jesus written across their lives. I believe that they will stand the test just like pillars in a magnificent building!

'Oh, why did I leave **Laodicea** to the last? Better far to have stayed in Philadelphia!' I broke in. 'Laodicea? I hear that it's the wealthiest city in all Phrygia. The banks are prosperous, there is a substantial medical centre and a huge market-place. There's something wrong with the water supply though?' John replied, 'You are so right. I fear that I have failed this Church. The perils associated with apostasy are quite evident. There's an utter lack of fervour and the whole mass of them are lukewarm in their faith. They think they can take it or leave it: "don't worry about us, everything will turn out right in the end!" Their pockets are full, the "purse" of their soul is empty. They are pathetically poor. I have endeavoured to counsel them to purchase "pure gold— refined in the purifying work of Christ." They will not listen. Such advice makes no sense to them: they prefer to trust their bankers. They are spiritually blind but don't perceive their cataracts: their eye specialists will deal with any short-sightedness! They need to gain the vision that focusses on right living! They pride themselves with their lavish garments. Why can't they see the need of making a change into the "garments" of spirituality? They need to accept the only way into Heaven— a personal relationship with Christ is the CRUX of the issue. They need to open the door of their heart and invite Christ in to abide with them.

'That's about it, Manaen. I feel as though I have done a trek throughout the entire region tonight but this evening's chat has clarified a lot of issues for me. I have a feeling that one day the Lord will require me to "stand up" to the problems pertaining to these churches for He has revealed the nature of what impedes the progress of each. He will make me ready, without a doubt, for the greatest challenge He has yet to place in my hands. Already He is placing it in my mind and heart. Let's call it a day—a night, more like it. We will rest well tonight I think.'

As I retreated into our room where Maryam was already sound asleep, I found myself agreeing with John and realising, also, that the descriptions he gave to that cluster of Seven Churches was really a description of the Church in any place at any time. What of the future, then? What of, say, ten or twenty centuries or more down through the corridors of time? Would it be possible, in an undreamed-of future, to recognise similar centres of religious fervour, of faithful adherence, or blasé blather, cold orthodoxy, friendly openness, or *laissez faire* somnolence—will they still be evident? I tend to think that nothing really changes but for the grace of God.

John was, almost, at the conclusion of his respite from that

ceaseless trekking through the territory of the Seven Churches—
I wondered if it was this seven-fold route that bonded the figure
seven to John's structuring of all things spiritual. Certainly, it was
the number so distinctive in *YHVH–Elohim's* planning in the
forming of this universe. John was still in our home at Antioch as
I came up to the conclusion of the series titled "The *In*-look on
Life". How very timely! 'John, I pulled together this final subject
in the series from previous discussions we have shared. I can't
think of a better way to present the topic than to have you at the
helm.' John smiled his approval.

To provide an adequate report on the content of that blessed
occasion, I will return to the outline and add the input of John
bar Zebedee to the proceedings so that I may recall the wealth of
discussion that erupted from each aspect of his discourse:

WHAT DO YOU EXPECT IN THE ETERNAL DAWN?
This is what Heaven will be like

1   AN OPEN DOOR INTO ETERNAL SPLENDOUR
    The transcendence of Time and Space: the limited will become
    limitless.
    John:
    Let me take you into the Upper Room where that Last Supper was
    held. So many unforgettable things were said. I will share a few…
    Of most significance for this class was the promise:
    'I go to prepare a place for you and I will come again to receive you
    so that, where I am, you may be also. The way you already know…
    I am the Way, the Truth, and the Life. No one comes to the Father
    without My guidance.'

2   SEE JESUS FACE TO FACE
    Receive His welcome smile as you enter your prepared Home
    John:
    I well remember Jesus' smile. It is so very familiar to me.
    From that very first day when He called me away from the fish, to:
    that horrific death scene at Calvary,
    the Resurrection morning,

the reunion at Galilee... the Ascension... Pentecost...

3   GAIN ETERNAL LIFE
We HAVE Eternal Life. In Heaven it is consummated
There will be no sickness, suffering, death
John:
It was the Lord who, personally, gave to me these amazing words:
God loves the world so very much that He was willing to offer His
only Son so that—through his death—no one who believes in him
will perish: they will HAVE everlasting life!
What we experience of Eternal Life today is but the foretaste of
what we will enjoy in Heaven.

4   THE MEETING WITH LOVED ONES
The reunion of family, friends, who have gone on before us
John:
I was inseparable from James, my brother. We grew up together,
went to the rabbinic school at Capernaum, worked for our father—
Zebedee—on Galilee, became involved with the Essene community
near the Dead Sea. Close by is the mouth of the Jordan River.
That's where we met with Jesus. Our lives were changed. We became
disciples then apostles but—so very soon—my own brother was
assassinated at the point of a sword.
One day, I will meet him again! And my parents, my friends.

5   RECOGNITION OF THE MARTYRS
Observe their honoured place in the Avenues of Heaven
John:
Manaen knew Stephen. He was the first of the Christian martyrs.
I understand that Nicolas—one of the original "Serving Seven"—
works here with his 2nd "Serving Seven", named "The Stephenos" in
honour of that great man. He was the first but, by no means, the last
of the Christian martyrs.

6   RECOGNITION OF BIBLICAL CHARACTERS
Abraham, David, Isaiah... Recognition comes through familiarity
John:
Let's have a response from the group. Who would be the very first
Biblical character you will want to meet in Heaven? What would you

wish to ask that man or woman? There's time to chat a while!

7   FIND YOUR NAME IN THE BOOK OF LIFE
A place is reserved for all: all who believe in Christ shall not perish
John:
*There is your name! If there is a space beside the signature, what
would you like to see written down by way of information regarding
your spiritual life and your daily witness?*
Never you mind! It's not the expertise of your service that counts!
It's a matter of recognition: does Jesus know you–do you know Him?

*On that grand and glorious Day
We shall see Jesus face to Face and we will tell the story:
SAVED BY GRACE!*

19. IS THIS OUR SON?

How quickly the seasons change. The weather was informing
us that there was a lessening of the chilly blustering of winter. A

bud or two were burgeoning on the parkland blossom trees. There was a pleasantness in the early dawn. This was no reason for that rapping on the door. 'Maryam! Who could be calling? Where is my cloak?

'Joy! Oh joy! Maryam! Come! Quick!' I hugged the young man and felt the tears flow. 'Papa, Emi, it's me. I'm home.' We looked at him, studied him—Onesimus, our new son. None the worse for wear, it seems. Oh yes, there was a weariness, though, easily explained by his sea voyage. There would be much to tell, more than we could ever have anticipated. His news would have to wait. 'Breakfast first, my lad and then we shall listen to your tales from here, there, and everywhere!'

Onesimus was hungry enough and attacked his meal with a furious intent. We smiled at him, rejoicing in the sight of him. 'No, no, Son. The dishes can wait. They are not for you today! Come, sit with us. What is the news of Paul? How is Dr Luke?'

'The thing is, Papa, Emi, I have not been with them for some time. I have been to Colosse!' 'What are you saying? To Colosse? How come?' He grinned that infectious grin of his. How pleased he appeared to be with his news. 'Why, on earth, have you been to Colosse?' And he told us his astounding story!

'Papa, I had been attending to the needs of Paul. Oh, let me first of all report that he continues to languish in the dungeon at Herod's Palace in Caesarea. What a place it is. Lavishly turned out above, brutally foul below! I cleaned his cell and made things more habitable. As the months went by, I came to the point of surrendering my secrets. Yes. I explained my years of slavery. I owned up to the location of my servitude. My home town is near Colosse.

'Paul knows Colosse. He had me pen his letter to the Christians there. And, Papa, Paul has actually included my name in his letter to the Colossians. My name is recorded there for all to see! I will be known; I'll not be forgotten on the refuse heap of life!

'He wrote another letter in his own hand. I have it here.' With each of his admissions, our eyes were growing wider yet! Onesimus unrolled the parchment with surprising tenderness! As he did so, his final admission came. 'When I told Paul the identity of my master, he jumped for joy—so much that his chains jangled! He knew the man. His name is Philemon. Paul explained that Philemon had received the Gospel, had become a Christian, was a changed man. The brutality had gone. He was now a generous, understanding man with a new-born kindness that would welcome and forgive me for absconding into Antioch!

'Paul advised that I return to my Colossian roots and own up to my own new found faith.' 'Onesimus! You mean...?' 'Yes, Papa, I have opened up my heart to the Lord. I am a Christian—body, mind and now: in my soul!' Words cannot adequately convey our joy at this news. Our boy, our son, continued his account of the events that brought him home—to Colosse, and then to us! 'Paul wrote to Philemon and vouched for me. Philemon welcomed me. Listened to me. Read Paul's document. Accepted it and me! Papa, Emi, Philemon has freed me from my slavery! I am a free man! He gave to me the letter Paul had written on my behalf. This is the letter!'

The document was spread out before us. Oh yes, it was from Paul!

Paul
A Prisoner of Jesus Christ
And Timothy, our brother
At Caesarea

To Philemon,
Dear friend and fellow worker
To Apphia, our sister,
To Archippus, our fellow soldier
And to the Church that meets in your home:

I always thank my God as I remember you in my prayers, because I hear about your faith in the Lord Jesus and your love for all the holy Community of Faith... Your love has given me much joy and encouragement.

We read on. I was fascinated by Paul's diplomacy, so evident in this letter to a new-born Christian—so very fitting and prudent as he set out to plead the cause of Onesimus.

I could, of course, order you to treat your one-time slave in the manner befitting Christian principles. Instead, I appeal to your good judgement as I am now an old man and a prisoner because of my faith in Christ.

Onesimus is like a son to me. He has been of invaluable service. How I would like to have him remain with me. It will tear my heart to see him leave. He's really taken your place in terms of assisting me.

Now Paul was shaping his letter to appeal to the very best in the heart of Philemon. 'Read on, Onesimus, read on.'

As I do not wish to retain Onesimus without your consent, he is returning to you in order that your decision concerning him will be spontaneous and decided upon with grace. This forced separation may well have been the means whereby you could no longer look upon him as a slave but be able to receive him as a brother in Christ.

If your view is that of continuing kindness, you will welcome Onesimus as you would me. If there is any debt relating to this matter, you have my word. I will repay the amount in full. The guarantee of this is in the fact that I am writing this letter to you by my own hand. (Not an easy task as you already know).

The beauty of Paul's wording bears down on our hearts. We realise that it was costing him much in ways more precious than any coinage—be it silver or gold!

Please, Philemon: refresh my soul. I have written to you in this manner for I am confident that you will receive Onesimus now as your brother in Christ and that you will be able to do even more than I ask of you.

And, one thing more: Please prepare a guest room for me as I intend to come to Colosse as soon as I am free of these chains.

Finally, dear friend, I include greetings from my fellow missionaries. Epaphras (who is also in chains with me here in Caesarea), also Mark...

'*MARK?* John Mark? Our John Mark? How is it possible?' Onesimus explained, 'Mark has been a most valued assistant now for some considerable time. He does much fetching and carrying. He carries letters here and there as Paul completes an epistle to the various churches he has raised in the name of Jesus our Lord. And, I think he is currently on his way to the church at

Thessalonica.' Can there ever be an end to the rejoicing that was welling in our hearts. Paul signed off with:

The grace of the Lord Jesus Christ be with you.

'Papa, Emi, the reason why I am here today is because, when Philemon saw my adoption certificate, he said that I must return to you with his blessing. When he handed this letter back to me, he said that, although it was of great value to him, it would be of even greater value to me. There is only one thing that I value more—except the love of my Lord and of my parents—it is...' Before the lad could pull it from his pouch, I had my half in my hand. With due solemnity, we joined the severed white stone so that—on the day of our reunion, we could rejoice in view of it.

'I see that you are carrying a parcel under the security of a seal, Onesimus.' 'It is of great importance, Papa, but let's not speak of it today. I would, so much, like to rest. And there are friends I must "inspect". The grin had returned. We let it be. Both Maryam and I were so elated with the events of the morning that we all felt in need of rest.

We went with Onesimus to the meeting hall that day and joined in all the happy hugging and back slapping that engulfed the gathering. Demetrius went off to gather up Astrid as she should not miss out on all the doings of the day. Eustace and Angela were somewhat hindered by the playful toddler—Eustace, son of Eustace—hanging about their feet. Nicolas was truly elated with the news of Paul's reunion with John Mark as were the Council members, Ambrose requesting a detailed report. The celebrations continued until the westering sun informed us that it was time to find our own homes once more.

After all the usual happenings of the morning had been attended following a satisfying night's rest, Onesimus sat with us to explain the nature of the parcel in his care. He lifted the substantive article for our scrutiny after requesting that we sit at table with him. The seal was broken as our son explained that the enclosed parchment was in his care because he was to deliver its contents to the Church in Rome!

Maryam and I were staggered. 'But, Onesimus, should you be breaking the seal if you are the courier of this parchment to Rome?' 'Indeed, I can, Papa. Paul has given permission. In fact, he has asked that I share its contents with you. He says that he would feel the better for your discerning eye upon the epistle.' We relaxed and commenced our intrusion into the precious document.

The epistle commenced, though not in Paul's handwriting, with his name and a brief introduction in which he mentioned having been aware of the Roman Church through Aquila and Priscilla. Paul then launched into his bold outline of the Faith he preached. For memory's sake, I made some brief notes:

PAUL'S EPISTLE TO THE ROMAN CHURCH

APOSTOLIC MANDATE:
>   Chosen by God to preach the Good News of the Gospel
>   This not new news. Prophets foretold coming of Messiah: Christ

THE DISTRESS OF THE LORD
>   The guilt of humankind—evil flung in face of God
>   When the Truth is known, there is no excuse for wickedness

GOD'S RIGHTEOUS JUDGEMENT
>   The Jews were entrusted with the revelation of God
>   Gentiles have a law: it is written on their hearts

JEWISH LAW
>   Law is their big boast: they can guide the spiritually blind!
>   The Jew is no guidepost if inner life is stained with sin

RIGHTEOUSNESS
>   The Jews: God's special people
>   The Lord needs faithfulness as well as lawfulness

IS THIS OUR SON?

HOW THINGS ARE MADE RIGHT
We cannot boast of having the answer: no works can save
Is the Law redundant? NO! Faith will uphold the law

EXAMPLES OF FAITH
Abraham trusted God and this was accounted as righteousness
The plan is to live by faith and so receive the free gift of grace

BEING MADE RIGHT WITH GOD
When we were helpless, Jesus came at the right time to die for us
Wages of sin: death! The gift of God: Eternal Life in Christ

THE RELEASE
Is the Law a sin? Never! Sin not known but for the Law
Who can deliver us? Thank God: Through Christ we are made alive!

FREE AT LAST FROM CONDEMNATION
The life-giving Spirit sets us free from the Law of sin and death
What the Law couldn't do, Christ achieved: He imparts new life

THE VICTORY IS OURS THROUGH CHRIST
Who or what could ever separate us from God's love?
Nothing! No one—in any circumstance—can sever that relationship

GRIEF AND GLORY
The grief: Israel is not saved!
The glory: God pours His grace upon us though we don't deserve it

UNIVERSAL SALVATION
The message must be proclaimed: the Gospel has gone into all the world
Faith has come through listening and believing

THE CULMINATING RESULTS
Has God cast Israel aside? Never!
The day will come: Israel will be grafted into the "tree" God grew

THE LIVING SACRIFICE
It's not the daily sacrifice that God requires, it is the *living* sacrifice

Be not conformed to worldly ways: be transformed into a new person

CHRISTIAN BEHAVIOUR
Love sincerely, be affectionate, diligent, steadfast, fervent, rejoice
Put aside all deeds of darkness. Look to the Light!

MINISTRY TO THE GENTILES
Christ confirms the promises made to the Patriarchs:
He also came to allow the Gentiles to place their hope in him

Some final matters of a practical nature and the intimation of Paul's desire to go to Rome and then fulfil a plan to journey on to Spain rounded off what I saw to be a monumental description of the Gospel. This document is perhaps the greatest coverage of Christian theology yet to flow off the pen of any man. It could be a worthy inclusion in the steadily expanding archives that hold the hope of an eventual *New* Testament! Paul's use of Isaiah's prophecy is so pertinent for here the Scriptures declare:

From the Root of Jesse shall spring up the One who will rule the nations and the Gentiles will place their hope in Him. (Isaiah 11:1).

"Tenacity" Auburn Road, Hawthorn, Victoria, Aust.

IS THIS OUR SON?

Paul's final prayer—in his own hand—blessed our souls:

Now to Him who is able to establish you by the Gospel and the proclamation of Jesus Christ—according to the mystery once hidden but now revealed so that all nations might believe and follow Him—to the only wise God be glory forever.

It was not possible to retire from these events and the enrichment of Paul's great treatise without seeking the assistance of my now somewhat battered writing kit. Certainly, it was showing the effects of great age and uncountable occasions of being called into service for the recording of soul-thoughts that escape into the poetry of a hymn. And it was so tonight. One could never forget that powerful clause which brought forth the spontaneous "Hallelujah" from a praising heart!

THERE IS NO CONDEMNATION
(Tune: *Penlan* 7.6.7.6. D, Iambic. Romans 8)

There is no condemnation
For those in Jesus Christ;
Through Him, God's Holy Spirit
Has set us free to trust!
We do not live the world's way,
We are aligned to grace;
Our minds are on His motives,
Our hearts know life and peace.

We're led by God's own Spirit,
We are His children here,
We ask our "Abba", Father,
To cast aside our fear!
The Holy Spirit counsels
That we are heirs with Christ,
For, if we share His suffering,
Also, we'll share His rest!

All wait in expectation
To see God's glory rise;
For any present burden
Cannot outweigh His grace.
And all creation waits still
To overcome decay,
While we await redemption
To the Eternal Day.

Our hope is without measure,
And unconfined, God's aid;
His Spirit helps our weakness,
He prays at God's own side!
What, then, are our responses?
If God is for us: Praise!
For none can separate us;
We're more than conquerors!

....

20. SPOKEN! IN EVERY AGE

Next morning, breakfast was on the table as Maryam and I surfaced. Grand and glorious occasions like the return of a son with his white stone, and the soaring thoughts of a powerful theological treatise such as that shared with us last evening, leaves the aging frame in need of rest! The aroma of breakfast caught up with us but also the devastating sight of bags packed, near the door! Onesimus must be on his way. Rome was calling: the parchment must be delivered. Rome had need to know the contents of that profound epistle! We could not wish it otherwise.

'Papa, Emi, do you think that you could come to us—the Church—in Rome?' 'Rome? It is so very far away and we are not as spritely now as when we came to Antioch. That voyage to Philippi had us literally on our backs!' 'But, Manaen,' it was Maryam, 'we would wish to see our son again. Let's think on it.' And think on it we did but, in the end, all matters other than the impending farewell of necessity pushed all such thoughts from our saddened hearts.

After his departure, many thoughts of Onesimus continued to crowd into our conversation. But eventually, I turned to face the inevitable. There was a course of study to prepare, with an inescapable realisation that this would be the final theme that I would be offering to the Church at Antioch.

A certain restlessness was engulfing my beloved and me as the possibilities of an autumnal voyage westward loomed. My writing kit agreed with me! The course most appropriate with which to confront my long-term students would be both a reflection of past studies and a challenge to open up the ears of the heart to what is being said by God today. The pen now proved rather spritely as the curriculum emerged:

GOD SPEAKS IN EVERY AGE

THE BEGINNING CREATION

1st Day:	Let there be light
2nd Day:	Let the firmament appear
3rd Day:	Let the dry land emerge from the ocean
4th Day:	Let the sun, moon and stars shine on the Earth
5th Day:	Let marine and bird life come into existence
6th Day:	Let animal species of every kind be born AND Let Us—the Triune God—create human beings
7th Day:	I speak My blessing over the Universe: It is GOOD!

Notes

Recall: the 3 *bara* creations: 1. Matter 2. Multifarious life 3. Man
Consider: the various meanings of *yom,* day: 24 hours... Age... Eon
Reflect: In the beginning, ALL things were assessed by God as GOOD.

THE FIRST STEPS   GENESIS

CROSS ROADS

Adam:	Come, follow My guidelines for life
Adam and Eve:	Where are you?
Cain:	Where is your brother?
Enoch:	Come, walk with Me
Noah:	You will need a boat
Abraham:	Pack your bags
Jacob	Change your ways

Notes

Recall: In dire circumstance, know that all storms have a "use-by" date.
Consider: Conversation is for companionship, communication is for continuity, communion is for consecration.
Reflect: A trackless wilderness should not deter a pilgrim from venturing out into the unknown future to fulfil the goals God sets.

MIGRATION — EXODUS

Jacob:	I AM God: don't be afraid to go to Egypt
Moses:	Go! You are to lead My people
Moses:	Why are you doubting?
Moses:	Share My Law with the people
Aaron:	Make Me a Sanctuary
Miriam:	It's time you listened to Me
Caleb:	I will bring you home

Notes

Recall: Divine revelation will always relate to where we stand with God—personal experience attests to His guidance.
Consider: When Law is viewed as a joy to follow, grace has done its work.
Reflect: Any setting—creation or construction—may be a sanctuary when God is acknowledged there.

SETTLEMENT — JUDGES

Moses:	This is the land I promised on oath to Abraham
Joshua:	Be strong and very courageous
Israel:	I have given you the victory
Deborah:	Lead your warriors
Gideon:	Go in the strength you have
Israel:	Go, face your enemies
Samuel:	Listen

Notes

Recall: Wisdom advises that firm foundations—in people and nations—are required for quality living.

Consider: Each nation has distinguishing features that have potential to enhance and harmonise life.

Reflect: Towering character develops in moral fibre and in righteous behaviour.

MONARCHY	THE KINGDOM
Saul:	You will become a new man
David:	I have chosen you to save My people
Solomon:	You seek wisdom? You shall have it!
Rehoboam:	You'll reign over your heart's desire... *IF...*
Elijah:	Go, challenge the king!
Hezekiah:	Don't be disturbed, I will deliver you
Josiah:	Because you listened, you will live in peace

Notes

Recall: Those knowing, and following, the Good Shepherd will negotiate the valley safely.

Consider: The tallest tree with a faulty "head" gives no clear signs of direction.

Reflect: Those who dare to be different can inspire a desire for virtue.

PRECEPTS	POETRY AND THE MAJOR PROPHETS
Psalms:	Be still and know that I am God
Proverbs:	They who listen to Me will dwell in Peace
Isaiah:	Whom shall I send? Who will go for us?
Jeremiah:	Stand at the crossroads
Ezekiel:	Stand on your feet, I want to speak to you
Daniel:	Peace: be strong now
Nehemiah:	I will gather the people

Notes

Recall: A song is a Psalm when its music flows through the soul

Consider: Wisdom makes the most of life's circumstance—we learn by an analysis of experience. Allow experience to speak to mind, heart.

Reflect: Those who see beyond the nimbus clouds of doubt can perceive the LIGHT.

CROSS ROADS

PRINCIPLES   MINOR PROPHETS

Hosea: I will heal the waywardness
Joel: I will pour out My Spirit
Amos: Go, preach to My people
Jonah: Get up! Go and speak to the people of Nineveh
Micah: I will gather the Exiles
Habakkuk: The righteous will live by their faith
Zechariah: Go, tell the people to return to Me

Notes

Recall: The heritage of Israel reminds of the danger of walking a shadowy path when the sun would lead to home.

Consider: Those who aspire to the heights should be careful where they place their feet.

Reflect: Storms pass as rainbow light brings hope: the rainbow promises a new day tomorrow!

GOOD NEWS   THE GOSPEL

Shepherds: Come, see the Child
John: Come and see... follow Me
Andrew: Come, take the "Bread" I offer
Woman at well: Come, drink at My "well"
The "flock":   Come, all you who are astray
Peter: Come, take up your cross, follow Me
Believers: Come, inherit The Kingdom

Notes

Recall: Shadows abound on history's page but a gateway has been opened into Grace.

Consider: Life's direction, integrity and wholeness is sourced in Jesus, the Christ.

Reflect: Resurrection—out of the dead leaves of the past—new life emerges to meet the sun and: The Son!

WORLD MISSION   THE CHURCH

The disciples: Go to Galilee: I will meet you there
Peter: Go out from Jerusalem
Stephen: Go, serve the people
Saul of Tarsus: Go, preach the Gospel
Paul: Go, be a light to the Gentiles

Paul: Go, you must preach the Gospel in Rome
John: Go, record the revelations I will give you
Notes
Recall: Those who reveal their true colours will stand out in any crowd.
Consider: The "called" know when it is time to leave a safe harbour with the Gospel.
Reflect: The Scripture holds more than words on parchment—it carries the Mind of God.

THE LORD HAS SPOKEN
Are you listening? Am I?
I went to the place of prayer where the Lord spoke again to me:

THIS IS GOD'S WORLD
(Tune: *Saved by Grace* D.L.M.)

The Lord has loved His tranquil world,
Its mountain heights,
its earthly sights;
The Lord has made all things so well!
The world has shown
what God has done!
But now His world has lost its way—
All peace has flown,
all hope seems gone.
This world's true hope is in the Lord,
His wondrous love will win the world!

The Lord has loved this troubled world,
He gave His Son,
His only Son,
That all who would believe in him,
No more confined,
shall be redeemed!
We will not die—we'll live with Him!
The world needs faith
to walk God's path.

CROSS ROADS

This world belongs to God alone,
And all should know what Christ has done!

The Lord still loves this trampled world
And every soul
He would make whole;
The homeless poor, the famine bound,
The prisoner in
his cell of pain,
Have need of Christ, His words of life.
What will you say,
to souls astray?
This world is God's! In love He gave
His only Son that we may live!

The Lord will love this tragic world
Till wars will cease
in endless peace!
Still burdened souls are slaves to sin,
Still children cry
and millions die;
They need to know of Calvary!
Where will you go,
His love to show?
God loves His world: Good News now heed!
God needs our hearts, our hands, indeed!

This poem—this rendering of soul language—must have been forming deep in the recesses of my mind for a great length of time for, as I allowed it to spill out over the parchment, I felt somewhat refreshed. In a day when there was no outward hint of peace, I discovered that peace profound once more that is the gift of my lifelong Friend: *Yeshua*–Jesus. My thoughts have long outgrown the *kebaa–baa–baas* of my childhood and youth for I know Him now as "The Good Shepherd" who gave His life for this "aged lamb": ME!

I went to Maryam with the poem, together with the outline of my final series for my cherished students, before she slept. How blessed the hearts of those whose love stands the test of time, trial and trauma, and of those who are able to meld that love, not only in their arms but in their very souls! We embraced the ramifications of that love deep into the night. When morning came, we consolidated our resolve to fix our sights on Rome. And, meanwhile, we would give of our very best to our spiritual family: the Church at Antioch.

21. CAESAR'S FOLLY

Autumn was in the air, the sun still shone brightly into all things pleasant at Antioch but the days were drawing in. Maryam had concluded her work in the clinic, with the Church placing the responsibility of the day-to-day ministrations in the capable hands of Eustace and Angela. Nicolas would continue to give oversight to the enterprise. The Church Council, under the capable direction of Ambrose, was preparing for the transition of our academic enterprise into a new administration. Already, I was finding my way through the last phase of our final theme: "God Speaks in Every Age". The urge to obey His imperative to "GO" is bearing in upon me. How does one sense, hear, the Voice of the Lord? One knows, recognises, soul language!

The house will be handed back to the Church. It is thought that Demetrius and Astrid may find it to be a more practical home now that their own little family is pattering about the floor boards of their confined dwelling. We hoped that our home could indeed become their home!

How appropriate that, on that final morning in our precious meeting hall, I was able to challenge my cherished students regarding the speech of God. 'Are you listening? What is He saying to you? And, *you*?' My class was not at all surprised that, at the end, I had asked Maryam to sing—to a melody composed by Bernice—my challenge to the Church at Antioch. It was my final word to my own "adopted" family!

KNOWING, GROWING, SERVING, SHARING
(Tune: *Cwm Rhonda* 8.7.8.7.8.7. Trochaic—rep. last line)

KNOWING GOD, discern His blessings,
Seek His will, declare His word;
Learn the ways of God most precious,
Find Him near on faith's long road.
Search the Scriptures, find their meaning,
Speak of Him, let Christ be heard.

GROW IN GOD, grow deep through nurture,
There be nourished in the soul;
Grow in grace and in God's favour,
Reaching up to faith's great goal:
Grow the fruit of God's own Spirit,
Fruit that is mature and whole.

SERVING GOD with heart and hand now,
Be alert to need and pain,
Take the tasks of lowly service
With no thought of earthly gain;
Hear the silent sounds of sadness,
Help souls to rejoice again.

SHARING GOD, reveal His power,
Power to conquer sin's demands
And reveal the transformation
When our lives are in His hands:
How the love of God has reached us
As His Kingdom now expands.

'Goodbye Ambrose, farewell Nicolas, Bernice; take care Eustace and Angela, Demetrius and Astrid. Farewell, all of our beloved family. There was a sadness upon us as we left them waving from the sanctuary.

As we reached the coast, it was pleasing to note all was calm. We embarked in anticipation of a placid crossing of "The Middle Sea". And once we had found our sea legs, so to speak, the voyage delighted us. Every effort was made by the sailors and servants to ensure our safe passage. One morning I braved the lowest deck where the oarsmen toiled their way against adverse currents, and lurching wood against the waves. With no respite, the *doulos* slaves continued on, their long days never eased until exhaustion called for another set of *doulos* men to make their way down into the depths of the hull.

Paul told me once that he considered himself to be a *doulos* slave: the lowest of the low. I hoped for him that—in his incarceration—Paul would not find himself swamped in the refuse of all that fell below the upper decks down to the hull!

There was no respite from the filth and grime of all that fell on the heaving shoulders of the *doulos* slaves! But Paul was, indeed, a *doulos* slave for Christ! I longed to see the one-time "Terror from Tarsus" so that I could observe those serving hands once more. He is my "Trusted Teacher" now! Certainly, the brilliance has not diminished—he had been nurtured in the peerless tutoring of none other than the greatest of all: Rabbi Gamaliel! Saul's lack of compassionate care had been transformed by meeting Jesus!

Would we ever meet again? Not this side of "Jordan", most probably. Maryam and I were sailing in "the placid lake" of the "Middle Sea"—the Mediterranean—and Paul was wallowing in the pit of the dungeon at Herod's Palace in Caesarea. Perhaps, when reunited with Onesimus, we may gain some news of Paul.

We were now sailing far west of our previous reach of the world's land and seascapes and soon the island of Malta would emerge from the western mists. This will be a new world opening up to us... How would we find the circumstances on this island, isolated as it is from the lands to its north, south, east and west? It was in our planning that we should stay a while, take in the sights and, if possible, it was hoped that we could speak our Gospel News to some of the Maltese population. Now, we were not so sure. However, as the ship docked, so must we for it was so recorded in the Captain's log.

We were able to stay on board overnight, however, and this stood us in good stead for we felt better able to meet the challenge of the day when the light of dawn softened the darkness of our cabin. Luggage received, goodbyes uttered and our gratitude accepted, we made our tentative steps up from the port and, thankfully, lodgings were found without much ado.

The morning was far spent. Food was in the offing after which, we decided to inspect the market place. There were the familiar aromas of the fish market; fruit was in abundance and... What's this? Purple drapery? Lydia? 'Lydia! Of all people one could expect to find on these foreign shores. Our good friend...' 'Manaen! Maryam—my dear, you look so well! You've just arrived? Let me close my store for the day. We must catch up with all your news. Why on earth do I find you here?' 'The same must be asked of you, dear friend,' I said with some glee!

As our lodging was nearby, we went there together with Lydia and sat under the awnings to imbibe a decent brew and chatter the day away with fervour and thankfulness in this unaccountable surprise. Here is Lydia, beautiful, gracious Lydia, drawing out our news and returning the compliment with us. Lydia had been asked to carry some purple cloth to Rome under Caesar's orders and she saw the good sense of plying her trade also in Malta on the way. How could it be possible—except in the Lord's scheme of things—that Lydia had booked to sail on to Rome in the same vessel as Maryam and I. How good is God?!

This day of our amazing meeting with Lydia was in no way

toning down. Great news was yet in store for us. Paul had passed through this very port! 'Paul? It must have been very recently. We would have received word, surely.' 'Come, friends,' Lydia replied, 'I will introduce you to Publius. He is the chief official on the island. He has excellent reasons for being aware of Paul's passage through Malta and for being amenable to all things Christian!'

What a superb setting, overlooking the sea. We were soon called back to reality by our host—Publius—for he was fair bubbling over with excitement. 'Friends of Paul? *Saint* Paul—the *hagios*, holy man of God? Come in, do come in!' Publius called for refreshments and sat us down in his garden that gave full range of vision down to the magnificent harbour below.

'Paul came to us from the sea—a boiling sea, a thunderous storm. It almost took the Roman crew, the cohort of soldiers guarding Paul and all the passengers: prisoners and otherwise. It had raged on for many days. All were without hope when the Lord intervened!' Joy! Oh joy! This man spoke of the Lord! Paul has been here!

Publius was now well into his account of fantastic happenings at sea! 'The storm did not abate for two weeks. There was no discernible difference between night and day. The prisoner took charge! He advised everyone to take some food— they'd need all their strength to reach the shore.

'Oh yes: all would be saved for the Lord had promised Paul that he would reach Rome to share the Gospel there! All cargo should be thrown overboard to lighten the load, he further advised. The soldiers had other plans. They purposed to kill Paul rather than have him escape. The centurion, however, stood up for Paul and warned his men against any such course of action. Paul would indeed reach Rome!

'Still in command, Paul gave further instructions. "Anyone who can swim take to the water and swim for that shoreline now in view. The rest of you, take a plank, a piece of this crumbling wreck of a ship and let it float you to the land!"

Publius continued, 'Upon reaching the beach—not so far from here, actually—a fire was kindled with everyone busily picking up stray bark and sticks. Paul did his best to cooperate until what was thought to be a fair-sized stick was actually a poisonous viper!' Maryam and I shuddered at the memory of the near demise of Astrid during that ill-fated youth camp at Antioch.

'The islanders who had gathered to observe the spectacle of Romans in such turmoil and distress, saw the viper clutch at Paul. "That proves the point," they said. "This man is a guilty murderer without a doubt. Saved from the waves but not judicial retribution!" Paul flung the reptile from his arm and went right on fulfilling the task assigned to him. "This man is no criminal... he is a *god!*" Our islanders bowed to him! (See Acts 27–28 for the story).

'Paul was then brought to my estate. I certainly welcomed him when told of his double indemnity! We celebrated for at least three days. My father took ill, suddenly. Paul went to him. Prayed for him. My father was healed! I tell you now, word got round and everyone, with ailments large or small, came to my estate and Paul ministered to them all. He took the opportunity also to tell us about *Christos*—Jesus, the Christ. All stayed with us for fully three months and we became a people now settled in this new form of faith. We honoured Paul and all the sailors until a ship that had wintered at the island was made ready to take them all, the sailors, soldiers and their prisoners, on to Rome.

'Lydia tells me that you and she are sailing on the rising tide on the morrow. I wonder if you would be able to meet with the local Church this evening? It is our usual study and discussion night. I understand from Lydia that you have been the leading teacher at the Church in Antioch.' 'Oh, certainly, I will be honoured to share my faith with the good people of Malta who have taken such good care of my greatly valued friend Paul!'

There was not much time to shake my brains into shape again following our relaxing voyage that was climaxed in the reunion with Lydia and then the amazing story surrounding Paul's visit to the island. It became quite clear that something of Paul's erudite sharing of his prolific understanding of the giving of God to all His people—Jew and Gentile alike—would be of utmost value here. But what to choose? It came to me: the gifts of God that are ours when taken from the open hands of *Yeshua*—Hebrew: Saviour, and *Christos*—Greek: The Anointed One. Paul had listed three great gifts that he intended to share with the Church at Ephesus. I inquired of my writing kit. Ah! my notes:

OUR SPIRITUAL BLESSINGS IN CHRIST

I must remember Paul's *Grace* and *Peace*: *"charis"* (grace) for the Greeks, *"shalom"* (peace) for the Jews. There is an evening's discussion filled up with just those two words. But Paul's preaching offers more than these. He stipulated that every spiritual blessing is available to us because God chose his people—Jew and Gentile—from before the foundation of the world to be holy and without blame—*hagios* and *teleios*—for He has adopted us into His family! This is not only according to His will but also for His good pleasure and because of His glorious grace. The group could rejoice in three of the resultant gifts of His grace.

These gifts we have through Christ:
WE HAVE REDEMPTION THROUGH HIS BLOOD
The forgiveness of sins is in accordance with His grace
God's redeeming grace is not deserved—
if deserved it would not be grace.

WE HAVE AN INCORRUPTABLE INHERITANCE
This inheritance was first disclosed to God's special people: Jews.
In Christ, all are included equally in this gifting: Gentile and Jew!
Consequently, we may call God "Father": *Our Father, who is in Heaven...*

WE HAVE A SEAL SECURING WHAT ONE DAY WILL BE OURS
Paul uses the word *arrhabon*—the "down-payment", the "engagement ring" that secures the whole! Today's experience of the Holy Spirit is the promise of all that is to come.

Therefore:
The riches of God's glorious gifting are available to all who are holy,
His incomparably great power is available to all who believe.

In retrospect, I have good reason to be thankful for the richness of Paul's ability to interpret the Scripture into the *lingua franca* of the people to whom it is given. The evening became an immense joy for—here I was—at the very forefront of the mission field trodden by the most intrepid of the Lord's warriors. A spiritual energy, coupled by the immensity of the opportunity had borne down upon me and the experience sent me finally to my lodging, hand in hand with Maryam, with a heart full of thankfulness.

The morning found us at the port awaiting embarkation. Everything seemed in order. Our luggage was already secreted safely and at last the order to board ship was given. Maryam and I, together with Lydia, clambered on board with as much alacrity as our aging frames allowed. I wondered then, would there be any obstacles ahead of us to keep us from our intended reunion with Onesimus? We were hopeful that the voyage would be uneventful. Let us not sail into any "cliff faces" of doubt, failures of faith, or trepidation of what lay ahead.

The Southern Ocean, via Great Ocean Road, Victoria, Aust.

As the weather was exceedingly pleasant, no gales arrived to deprive us of our somnolence and leisured conversation among our fellow voyagers. Our expectations regarding the immediate future were not far from the surface of our discussions, however, and many ifs and buts and whys and wherefores began to surface. Here was the coastline of the centre of the full power of the Roman Empire looming large on our horizon. What awaited us now?

'Look, Maryam, there is someone waving from the wharf. Could it be… Look, dear heart, it is! Onesimus! And there is also someone with him... I wonder... The inevitable jerk that sent a shudder through the vessel announced our arrival at the Port of Brindisi on the south east coast of Italy. Joy! Oh joy! Onesimus stood on the wharf waiting to deliver his greetings and to introduce the most beautiful companion one could wish to meet! My immediate employ, though, was to take hold of my belt pouch and extract my half of the white stone! Onesimus busied himself also with his pouch. "SIMON" was delivered to its "FIRST" half. We were whole again! United once more. It was hug time. Then, 'Onesimus, your friend...?' 'Papa, Emi, meet Maria.'

Our focus of attention, of course, was upon Onesimus and his companion. We almost missed the departure of Lydia. Thankfully, she came to us and, with much goodwill and good wishes, we took our leave but with firm promises to keep in contact whenever possible! We turned again to our son and to Maria.

There was an undeniable warmth in Maria's approach to us. 'Onesimus has told me much of you both—that you took charge of him when it seemed there was no possible way back from his living death. How happy I am that you gave to him a new chance, a new hope, a new life. And, he came to me. Papa, Emi—if I may call you that—thank you for making it possible for Onesimus, the love of my life, and me to meet, to find each other...' And all the while, Onesimus was smiling that engaging grin of his. Onesimus was pleased with life, was pleased to greet his parents and exceedingly happy just to allow Maria to present the facts. Onesimus was in love!

The horse-drawn carriage had arrived and the man in charge hastened us on board. Rome was, undeniably, still a great distance ahead of us. There would be ample time to swap and share the news of recent times as our carriage trundled its spectacular journey along the *Appia Antica*—the Appian Way. It was explained that this significant name was derived from the original builder, Appius. What a magnificent road this is to haste us on our way. This major thoroughfare was made from volcanic rock in parts and cemented to insure a smooth ride throughout the terrain. Originally a route prepared for the movement of Rome's military forces, the Appian Way has become the major route to the capital.

Never, in all our lives have we encountered such opulence as confronted us along this grand highway. Spectacular villas, imposing monuments and ample gardens eased the journey and we found ourselves on the city's outer limits without too many challenges. What had Onesimus prepared for us? We were confronted with the Catacombs of Rome!

Maryam joined me in a small alcove in a massive cavern where many people—babies, children, youths, the mature and the elderly—were becoming familiar with communal living at its most basic. Surprisingly, there was room enough and sheltered sufficiently to ensure our privacy with relative comfort and ease. It was noticed, also, that there was a steady flow of air—much cooler than the after-effects of the late afternoon's scorching sun across the city.

After the first shock in being confronted by such extreme conditions, with various vermin and sludge distracting us from a meagre measure of comfort, we agreed that, after all was said and done, the catacombs were, at least, a reasonably safe place to be—especially because we were sheltered from the ever-vigilant soldiers attending to Caesar's beck and call!

There was food enough and pleasant enough for us to be satisfied and, as we engaged in this repast, Onesimus and Maria took time to explain the setting and the circumstance in which we found ourselves. The catacombs, we discovered, are not a new phenomenon, necessitated by the whim of a mentally deranged ruler. Many, many years ago, the catacombs were first utilised as the caverns of the dead. Of necessity, they then became inhabited by Jews of the Diaspora when threatened with extinction. As their situation became less tenuous, the caves were abandoned until they became a place of refuge for the current inhabitants as the Christian population of Rome began to expand to a level most unpleasing to the ruling elite.

The Christian way of doing things, it was feared, would ultimately swamp Rome. Its power would wane and the followers of "The Nazarene" would take over the world. They threatened to do so by the plethora of "Jesus" propaganda floating about the capital and every hamlet from the west to east of the Empire. Christianity's fate was sealed—presumably!

'Where are you living? Are you safe?' 'Oh yes. Maria has her personal place in an alcove set aside for maidens and I bed down with the youths—a noisy, pillow fighting bunch but we get on well and we also get on with the work required to keep this community functioning satisfactorily.'

'Papa, you and Emi will need at least a day or so to become acclimatised. A morning stroll in the near neighbourhood wouldn't go astray either. We are relatively safe here for the time being though Caesar is broadening his powers over us. I want to take you to Peter as soon as possible, though. John Mark is with him now. Paul gave him leave as it seems that Mark has a special project for which Peter can give best support to him. Something about a history; he said that you would know about his work. Although presently under surveillance, Paul is free to receive visitors and he is longing also to see you!

'Beside all of that, Maria and I have waited for your arrival. We are pledged to each other and we want no further delay in our plan to marry. Papa, I have asked Peter to marry us according to the way Christians perform such ceremonies here. I see that you are disappointed but, Papa, I want you to stand at my side. You are my best friend as well as my Papa! Would you do that for me? You know that I will want a song prepared for us and for you to pronounce a benediction over us. Can we start to plan the day now?'

The glory that is Rome spread out before us. A magnificent array of towering grandeur confronted us as we took that promised stroll with Onesimus and Maria. Not yet our daughter by law, Maria already is so integral to the happiness exuding from Onesimus that we were experiencing a new sense of family. As we walked, and talked, much was learned about the current status of Christians in Rome.

For some years' past, the Community of Faith had burgeoned into a substantial enterprise where spiritual values are deemed as paramount, placing political machinations into correct perspective. Caesar was not impressed! The iron force of the Roman Empire has now been bearing down on us with ever greater intensity. 'This is the reason why we have taken to the catacombs,' Maria explained.

We are informed that Maria was born into Rome's high society, among the rich and famous, but she was required to sever all family ties when she committed her life to Jesus. Every economic advantage renounced, Maria began to walk among the Christian Community and found her new family! Maria also found Onesimus. What a team they will make!

'Onesimus, take me to Peter. We can plan for your wedding

there and then, I must take time to observe what Mark has already achieved with, how did you put it—with his "history". It will be more than a history, Onesimus. It will read much more like a diary! You see, John Mark knew Jesus personally while still in his teens. He can tell "The Jesus Story" from an eye-witness point of view. And Peter can fill in all the missing details. Mark was never in Galilee, you see. He will need to hear what Peter has to say. Obviously, that is happening now!

'Peter! Peter! Wonderful! A lot of silver strands in hair and beard, I see—who am I to comment on the facts? Look at you, Peter. The boisterous fisherman has become the sainted sage— the holy man, different from those of the world all around you and making a difference that will count down all the centuries to come! Peter, I do hope that the true meaning of the word *hagios*—holy (saintly)—will never be labelled exclusively for those "gone on before". We are to be holy men and women in the world today. Otherwise, the power of our witness will be lost. We must, in word and deed, reveal a difference from that of sin-stained humanity so that we may make a difference in the lives of those to whom we bring the Gospel—the Good News. The saints live today!'

'Mark, come. Quick, now. You'll never guess who's here!' 'Manaen! Wonderful! Let me look at you. None the worse for wear, I see!' Mark's excitement was a joy to behold. We had to catch up with one another's news, of course. Then I was able to fill Mark in on the recent state of the work in Antioch. We spoke of Nicolas, Demetrius and Astrid, Eustace and Angela. Their growing families were included. We shared our views on the much-venerated Ambrose and his team. Mark was now "up to date" with the evolving ministry in Antioch.

In turn, Mark described the change in his relationship with the Apostle Paul. It had been of immense worth to Mark to be so closely involved in Paul's "world-wide" ministry. He had been a courier on a number of occasions. But Paul knew of Mark's obligation to my on-going project to provide an extensive coverage of the birth, growth and development of the Christian Church. The Community of Faith, first named "Christians" in Antioch, was now recognised as such in so many enclaves around the Jewish, Greek, and Latin arenas of the world. The Church was going "global"!

'Bring me up to date with your written work, Mark.' He responded happily. 'Because I commenced this endeavour in response to your challenge, I do not have to describe the focus points in my narrative. So, to begin: because I grew up in Jerusalem, I was tutored at the Temple's Rabbinic School, as you know. How fortunate for, as a lad, I became quite sensitive to all the hints in the ancient scrolls concerning the *Messiah* who was to be the Saviour of the world. Why didn't our people recognise Him when he came, Manaen?

'I was hungry to learn more about the *Messiah* and, as a Jew who believed in *YHVH*–LORD, I felt drawn particularly to the way *Yeshua*–Jesus offered up his life as a sacrifice so that, by his death we may find Eternal Life. Paul has been of great assistance to me, Manaen. You know that my early defection from the first missionary journey infuriated Paul. He wanted nothing more to do with me. But his disappointment has turned into an appreciation of my work with him.

Paul actually asked for my assistance and now declares that I have been very useful. It has been with Peter, though, that allowed my pen to flow more fluently! Peter is filling up all the missing gaps in the record. And there are some events that I have been able to describe fully myself, including that ghastly event in Gethsemane! When you are able to read my manuscript, you will see that I do present *Yeshua*–Jesus as the Saviour of the world.'

'I am most impressed with your endeavours, Mark. Keep it up. Don't allow the ink to run dry! Let it flow, along with your inspiration. Your work will stand the test of time. As for Maryam and me, we will continue to support your endeavours as best we are able. I'm going to meet with Paul now. Do you have a message for him?' 'Please let Paul know of my progress with the project and that I will visit him soon.'

'Manaen! You've come. At long last, you have finally arrived in Rome! How good it is to see you. Please, how is Maryam?' 'Paul, Paul, my "Trusted Teacher", how...' 'Teacher? No! if anything, I am the prophet—the proclaimer, the preacher if you would prefer! You are the teacher, Manaen. You were already a teacher when a student at the Rabbinic School in Jerusalem! And look at the years of your ministry to the Church at Antioch. I hope there is some energy left to share your mountain of knowledge with the Church in Rome.

'I hold grave fears for the future of our enterprise in Rome, Manaen. The storm clouds are gathering. We have but little time to share our faith in this hub of atheistic anarchy! I know, I know: there is the mighty iron fist and force of Caesar's armies but, look around you. Where do you find stability?'

'My friend, I sense that our time is short. But Caesar will never be able to quash what has been commenced here in Rome. We are hounded, yes; threatened, certainly! Cowered? No! Thwarted? Never! But the night is coming when we will be unable to do the work to which we are called. You and I are almost spent as far as physical energy is concerned so we must set about preparing the next generation to take hold of the challenges, carry the burdens and continue with the seeding, the cultivating, the harvesting of the "golden grain" in the seasons yet to be.

'Our task is to enthuse the workers to pick up their spades, till the ground, root out the weeds, nurture the "crop" with good "food", sufficient watering and adequate weathering. Manaen, come again. And soon. I need your assistance in what I consider will be the final work the Lord is placing in my heart and hand!'

In returning to the catacombs, I found Maryam much in need of my company. I had been away for some time and this was hardly fair to my beloved. We reclined on a reasonably comfortable and substantial couch. I brought Maryam up to scratch as it were with the happenings of the day, sharing my observations concerning Peter, John Mark and Paul who had sent his personal greetings to her. We wondered to what it was that Paul was alluding in speaking of his "final work". Conjectures were not good enough. We would have to wait. Besides, there was a wedding to consider and, when Onesimus and Maria returned with an evening meal, we four finalised the wedding plans.

Maria's family would be conspicuous by their absence but her new family would be much in evidence. Onesimus would have the full support of his own family: just the two of us. But Onesimus maintained that it was not the numbers but the quality of his family that counted with him. Besides, his youthful friends of the catacombs would be much in evidence. John Mark would arrive with Peter and, though Paul was living under the restrictions of Rome, his presence would be replaced by a wordy message to be read from the hand of the groom's "best friend" and Papa: me!

Though I would have wished to be the officiating celebrant on this splendid occasion, I was much placated by the fact that I stood beside our son as he and Maria exchanged their marriage vows. Through good or ill, riches or poverty, sickness or health, he and his bride were to be one and their union would not be severed in any circumstance.

How does one negotiate such a wonderful occurrence without a deep sense of emotion? Onesimus had requested a marriage hymn. He and Maria would receive a prayer song never before heard or sighted, save by one: at the time, my bride of one night.

As Maryam rose to sing the prayer I had written for her, I heard again the mellow tones of her beautiful voice, though now somewhat tremulous today for she had just opened her now faded parchment to express its sentiments:

THE WEDDING HYMN

(Tune: *The greatest of these*)

Day of rejoicing,
Moment of blessing,
Hour when are sanctified
The vows of love's union
Sealed at this altar,
Heart and hand for e'er entwined.
What shall I pray for you,
How shall I speak for you?
O LORD, this marriage bless;
Grant each Your guidance,
Enduring patience:
O LORD of love,
Grant faithfulness.

Day of enrichment,
Moment so hallowed,
Hour when the future is sealed;
How swift will time fly
Into tomorrow:
For that day is grace revealed.
This shall I pray for you,
Here will I plead for you:
May grace outweigh your cares,
Hope bring you courage,
Faith be your anchorage:
His Love Divine,
This gift God shares.

Day for remembrance,
Moment enduring,
Hour when we celebrate
A dawning future

Rich in love's sharing,
Radiating Heaven's own Light.
This would I speak for you,
As now I pray for you:
O LORD, Your aid bestow,
By Your own virtue
This union nurture;
Abiding love,
These lives o'erflow.

Day of commitment,
Moment compelling,
Hour of love's pledging complete,
As vows well cherished,
Spoken before Him,
Echo now in lives replete.
Here will I speak for you,
Now make my prayer for you:
May peace attend your ways,
Joy meet your morrow,
Soothe every sorrow;
Eternal Love,
Grant love always.

It was from a thankful heart that I pronounced the Aaronic Benediction (Numbers 6:24–26):

THE BLESSING OF THE LORD BE YOURS,
THE BLESSING OF HIS GRACIOUS WAYS,
THE BLESSING OF HIS SHINING FACE,
THE BLESSING OF HIS COUNTENANCE;
HIS GLORIOUS LIGHT NOW SHINE ON YOU
AND GRANT TO YOU HIS PERFECT PEACE.
AMEN, AMEN, AMEN.

The long years of our own marriage fled past me now and I found myself in the grip of a memory that will never dim. The Lord has blessed our union and, as Maryam gave expression to that sacred memory, my own thoughts were captured by our first embrace.

Following the resultant festivities and the multitudinous speeches, hand-clappings and good wishes, we allowed Onesimus and his bride to depart. The community revealed the depth of their love for the pair by having secured some suitable, private accommodation that had been prepared especially for them. But we would see the happy, wedded couple again quite soon!

....

22. SEIZE TODAY

It was time to return to Paul. The months were fleeting fast! The sight of his prison-weary face filled me with some alarm. Things were pulling themselves into an inevitable conclusion for us as the years were upon us in large measure. What could possibly be the nature of the enterprise Paul had in mind? I took the precaution to take with me the two most precious... hmm, how does one give expression to the identities here? Oh, that must be it: the two most precious *identities* in my present care. Undoubtedly, first and foremost: Maryam—I was not going to leave her stranded in the catacombs while I enjoyed a special time of collaboration with Paul again—and my aged writing kit: the *bar mitsvah* gift from my parents: Yehudith and Baruch of Bethlehem!

Paul seemed tired. He explained that some of the emperor's "insiders" had informed him that Caesar was preparing to ensure a greater security in the dungeon's prison chains once more. Oh yes, there are already Christians abiding in Caesar's household! Paul provided a detailed account of the tenuous situation at present encountered by Caesar's staff.

'My contacts inform me that Caesar is more prone to be plucking away at his fiddle than employing his fragile mind with the improbability of managing his empire. I fear for Rome. It could go up in flames for all he cares. And there would always be someone to blame... Christians, without a doubt of it. Oh, Caesar would point his fiddle-plucking finger at us. The man is a psychopath, a debauched tyrant who thinks nothing of those he sends to a crucifix—perhaps one day even Peter, or myself.

'There is no time to spare.' 'What is your project, Paul?' 'Manaen, we must go back to the beginnings!' 'The beginnings, Paul? I thought that Matthew, Mark, Luke and John also, are engaged in that enterprise.'

'Manaen, I have preached Good News on foot through many

"edge- of-the-world" climes and cultures, I have wielded my pen to the best of my ability so that the Romans, the Corinthians, Galatians, Ephesians, Philippians, the Colossians, those of Thessalonica and numerous others have received the Gospel by means of the written word. I have not spoken to our own people, Manaen—our people: the Hebrews! We must go back to our beginnings!' I caught his enthusiasm. 'When do we begin?'

'Manaen, both you and I had the very best of education in The Law during our years at the Temple's Rabbinic School in Jerusalem. Though widely divergent in our beliefs and attitudes—can we ever forget it—during those years, none-the-less, our grounding in the Faith of our Fathers was most comprehensive and compelling. It was only the meeting with Jesus that placed those tablets of stone into proper perspective.

'The Law is God's Law, not that of Moses. He was merely God's spokesman—and a stuttering one at that. The Law was intended to provide a knowledge between right and wrong. That knowledge, we found, was quite inadequate to change the pattern of our actual behaviour. We didn't know what sin really was until Moses pointed to those slabs. Israel must realise that slabs of stone do not bring about the miracle of a re-birth into the grace where we now stand! What do you say, my friend?'
'What a "turn-around" we had in meeting with Jesus,' I replied. 'Where do we begin?'

Paul went on to explain his reticence in commencing the project. 'No self-respecting, orthodox Jew is going to open up an epistle sent from the hand of one "Saul of Tarsus"! This work must remain anonymous. I can provide you with the outline but what I really need is for you to shape the content in a manner more conducive to a teacher's point of view. The vocabulary must be yours, not mine. Dr Luke or Apollos can then translate the textual material into Greek in order to allow for the Diaspora also to have access to the work. Because of our partnership, the authorship will remain unknown. But, Manaen, I will want the manuscript to actually be read! This is the only way.' 'Let's then, begin at the beginning! What we learned at the Rabbinic School in Jerusalem must not be forgotten but The Law must be placed in perspective so Israel will see not only the beginning but also the end: the completion, where Law is superseded by Grace!

'As you can well imagine, Manaen and Maryam, I have given much thought over the years to the paramount theme: it relates to human spirituality treasured with such intensity by the Hebrew people. This has been so since those wilderness years under the tutorage of *YHVH–Elohim* via the voice and slab-holding of Moses.

'I have managed to divide my thoughts into twelve main themes and rounding off with a few practical matters. So then, Manaen: to our beginnings!'

My battered writing kit set itself to be of service yet again. As Paul began his long-delayed treatise to his own people: Israel—known best through their long history as the Hebrews—I discerned a profound work evolving. I will record, briefly here, the major issues that emerged as Paul outlined the burden of his message to the Hebrews:

GOD'S WORD TO THE HEBREWS: ISRAEL

1   THE SUPREME REVELATION
    The Creator has spoken in many ways: through patriarchs,
    Prophets and in these latter days, God spoke through His Son

2   THE ACHIEVEMENT OF OUR SALVATION
    In the past sin had veiled the Truth
    How did the Gospel reach us? Through the Son being born human

3   THE FAITHFULNESS OF JESUS
    Moses was faithful to his father's house; Christ is Lord of the house
    We are that "house" if we hold fast our hope with confidence.

4   GOD'S PROMISES ARE SURE
    If you hear God's voice, do not block your ears!

CROSS ROADS

Let us come boldly into His presence to obtain His mercy, grace

5   JESUS: THE GREAT HIGH PRIEST
All aware of the obligations of the high priest: to intercede for all
Christ the High Priest appointed by *YHVH*–LORD

6   SPIRITUAL STAGNATION
The time has come to move on from elementary teaching of the past
We've always known about repentance: move on to the New Life

7   THE PRIESTLY KING: "*MELCHIZEDEK*"
Here is the personification of "The King of Righteousness"
Christ saves to the uttermost all who come to God through Him

8   THE NEW COVENANT
This is the crux of the whole narrative! God said (Jeremiah 31:33):
I'll place My Laws within your mind, write them upon your hearts.
I'll be your God, you will be My people. All will know Me: forgiven!

9   THE SANCTUARIES
The earthly sanctuary is indicative of how to worship
But there was no inner purity, so Christ came to cleanse our souls

10 THE DIFFERENCE IN THE SACRIFICES
A bull, a goat, cannot atone for sin. Not a yearly event: ONCE only:
It is by merit of Christ's blood that we enter the New, Living Way

11 SALVATION COMES THROUGH FAITH
What is faith? The source of hope, the evidence of things not seen
Without faith, it is impossible to please God

12 THE RACE OF LIFE
Look to the One who will finish, perfect, our faith
It was for the joy set before Him that Christ endured the cross

FINALLY: THERE IS A NEED FOR CHRISTIAN LOVE
Be hospitable—you may entertain an angel!
Remember: His grace is all you need

BE COMPLETE IN CHRIST

'I'm tired, Manaen. The strictures of prison life are sapping my energy. I'm weary, yet there is so much yet to be done. I've carried the Gospel to the Gentiles but the imperative weighed heavily upon me to address "home base" before the end of earthly things for me. You know it well: I sat at the feet, so to speak, of Gamaliel—none better to enforce the claims of the establishment. "Things must not change. And things pertaining to the Temple must *never* change."

'But things have changed, irrevocably for me. I have needed to speak to Israel. The Lord was impressing this burden deep in my soul and I felt that I didn't possess the *persona* whereby my voice would be heard in Israel. It is Israel that landed me in this stew and the pot is getting hotter. In those early days, I could let off sufficient steam from my own assessment of my capacities! Now, my fervour is focussed on fulfilling the ministry to which I was called when galloping with my murderous intent all the way to Damascus! How could I have guessed just where that road would lead after The Light shone on my path?

'Here I am in Rome, with a further clamp-down in a prison cell looming large. My dear scribes were waiting to record what must be said. Their pens were devoid of words! And then you came: your writing kit and you will see the Epistle to the Hebrews finally unsigned, but sealed and sanctified! No signature, mind you. Let the document speak for itself. It really carries the Lord's imprimatur. This will be enough to carry the Truth contained therein on down through the centuries. In the end, Israel will come to realise how faith in *Yeshua*–Jesus will transform God's very own, special people!' Manaen, come again if possible. Maryam, take care of him and yourself! And, wherever your feet may now fall, take my greetings with you on the way!'

Maryam and I were becoming more accustomed to our underground "home". Deep carved into the hills of Rome for the purpose of providing a burial place for the dead, the catacombs were proving to be a safe hiding place from the ever-threatening authorities. Generally speaking, Rome was tolerant of the many religions flourishing here. Christians, and the Jews, were out of favour though because they refused to give deference to Caesar as a god!

Soldiers seldom entered the catacombs. Though the interminable tunnels presented an unnegotiable maze, there were cryptic signs here and there to keep one on track. We had noticed, soon after our initial entry to "The Place of the Dead", that well-defined carvings of a fish were scattered about.

Closer inspection had determined that, indeed, the fish were placed in strategic positions. Not all the inhabitants of the catacombs were Christians. Absconding villains and malcontents also found the caverns to be a safe hiding place. The fish sign puzzled me. I asked about its significance. 'Because it is an *ichthus*, Manaen.' 'Yes, that I know: the Greek word for fish, but I don't understand the reason for its presence here.' 'It is a cryptic message, Manaen. It signs the way to the Christian areas of the catacomb.' 'How so?' I persisted. 'It is a proclamation of the Gospel, Manaen!' 'How so?' I asked again. And then my informant spelled it out for me:

I: *Iesous*, CH: *Christos*, TH: *Theos*, U: *Uios*, S: *Soter*.
JESUS CHRIST, GOD'S SON, SAVIOUR

'To those in the know, Manaen, the fish is as good as a signpost: "This way to the Christians".' Ingenious! Magnificent.

211

How could I ever face a fish again without a sense of joy at what it now conveyed.

'Maryam, there is a freshening breeze today. The season is changing. I wonder where Onesimus and Maria—beloved, you realise we have a daughter now—are today.' 'Wonder no more, dear heart, for here they are!' 'And don't they look pleased with themselves,' I added quite unnecessarily! Our greatest pleasure in these somewhat austere conditions in the catacombs was to sit with the newly-weds and speak of hopes, concerns, of faith and of future plans.

'Papa, Emi, we have news for you. We will be as you before the year is done. There will be a little one to call us "Papa, Emi" too!' I thought the alcove itself would explode with the news but not a clump of clay fell on us! Joy! Oh joy! Our present circumstance could in no way diminish the excitement in our "camp"! 'Papa, it has been decided that, if the bonny babe is a boy, his name shall commence with "M"'. Maria chimed in: 'And, if a little girl, her name shall commence with "M".' Onesimus picked up the threads again. 'There are no prizes for the one who could declare just what those names would be!' But, then...

'Papa—Pastor Pa, Mother: Emi, there is some further news. Maria and I have stood once more at the "cross roads". We have heard God calling us to take up our cross and follow *Yeshua*-Jesus westward, into Spain! We must move soon for we wish to find work for me and be settled before our little one arrives. We realise that we have come to the time of parting with you. Never out of mind, never squeezed from our hearts but your dear faces will be gone from us. Our true parents, we will never forget you.'

'And we have gained a son, a new son! Our family is growing—we have a daughter now and, one day soon, a little one to make of us grandparents! You are God's gift to us! We cherish you. We will mourn your parting from us but know that it is God's will for you!

Onesimus, you came to the "cross roads" of life. I met you there. I prayed for you there. You took the right road! We would not halt you in your tracks! You have come to know of Jeremiah, the prophet. Let his words be a benediction to your soul!

This is what the LORD says:
'Stand at the crossroads; seek the path that is tried and true;
ask your (soul Guide) to point you in the right direction and
choose to walk in it. You will then find rest in your soul!'
(Source: Jeremiah 6:16).

After they had gone to their own alcove, Maryam and I reflected on the years since Onesimus had burst in upon our lives. That destitute youth crouched and comfortless, wrapped about in a fetid, matted cloth, first found devoid of hope in a back lane of Antioch, has developed into a confident, intelligent and eloquent Christian. Here was a man now witnessing resolutely, through word and deed, to the utter commitment so profoundly upon him. And here was a couple with The Light kindled in their soul which would burn brightly through the years. The Gospel will gather strength in Spain through their endeavours.

'Maryam, we must leave this city. Rome is no dwelling place for us. Antioch is far away. Too far for us. I wonder, dearest one, if it could be of benefit if we removed ourselves to Philippi? We were happy there. The people gathered us to their hearts. And, Lydia is returning to Philippi soon. What do you say?' Maryam always speaks most eloquently with her eyes. They glowed. This had been a momentous day! We also had received news about our growing family. The white stone would have its uses again!

The bags were packed once more. We were not without friends in Rome for arrangements were made for us to vacate the city under cover of darkness. God's grace is always found to be sufficient, even in the most trying of circumstances. Of utmost importance to us was to ensure the embarkation of our family,

Onesimus and Maria and wave them on their westward way. We had determined that, when they had settled in their new environment, we would receive word of their address via the capable hands of John Mark. Onesimus would know his address in Rome, John Mark would know of ours in Philippi! We could communicate via the written word safely delivered by couriers.

There was a deep sadness upon us, though. Such farewells are beyond tears, they are secreted in the soul. We held to Onesimus and Maria for as long as the blaring horn of the vessel about to sail would allow. Beyond the sadness, there is still the joy! There is a light kindled in the hearts of Onesimus and Maria that dire adversity could not douse. And, as their ship set sail, we knew that no welling waves upon the winds of circumstance would deter them from their goal.

Farewell Onesimus, Farewell Maria. Go now to Spain. And what of the islands to the west of Spain? Would Britain come to a living faith in *Yeshua*–Jesus, the Christ? The answer lay beyond the waves of current circumstance. But, where there is a lighthouse of hope, the Gospel will be heard!

Exit from Macquarie Harbour, West Coast, Tasmania

'Maryam, where is my writing kit? There's something of importance that I must record before the ending of the day.

ALL TIME IS IN YOUR HANDS
(Tune: *Sagina* 8.8.8.8.8.8. Iambic—Rep. 2 last lines)

All time is in your hands, O Lord,
The past: our Heritage of Faith,
The present is our "Day of Grace":
The future is unknown to us
But we believe there is a place
For us beyond the days of Earth.

The world is in Your hands, O Lord,
This precious world, creation's flower;
And yet we see decay, discord.
In darkest night where sin has soared
And human grief sees grief outpoured,
We claim the Saviour's cleansing power.

Our life is in Your hands, O Lord,
And You have sealed us as Your own;
We trust Your ever-blessed Name!
From Heaven's Glory once You came
To die for us and take our blame;
You grant Your peace till Heaven is won.

Our hope is in your hands, O Lord,
We see Your loving care and know
That we can trust You, come what may.
We'll serve you till the end of day:
You are The Light, our shining ray,
And we will walk within its glow.

All grace is in Your hands, O Lord,
Your grace is multiplied by grace!
Abounding grace has set us free,
Through grace we'll live eternally,
There's grace enough for even me:
It is in grace we find our peace.

'Come, darling, Lydia is beckoning. I understand that we must go on board tonight for the ship sets sail on the rising tide. Maryam, your "princess pearls" are now almost all gone. They have been the means of keeping us afloat financially through all the years since our escape from Jerusalem. Those pearls have taken us to Antioch. They have enabled us to live comfortably in our home together with Onesimus.

'We had lost our son. But we have gained another. Now he has also gone from us. But Maryam, though we have farewelled him and Maria westward to Spain, we still hold him in our hearts. Come dear heart, we must rest.' Some hours later, we awoke to the now familiar sound of waves splashing rhythmically against the hull and robust sails straining against the mast. 'Maryam, let's go up on deck to greet the dawn.

'Look, there is a heavy mist and the early sun is almost obliterated. But see, the mist is carrying many golden rays of light almost into our hands. Oh, Maryam, see how those rays—like golden threads—are highlighting the morning. They certainly put the darker strands in their rightful place—amidst the clouds! Dear heart, these are so like the golden threads that have given the vital texture to the fabric of our lives.

We've known darker threads aplenty in the past and could name them each by circumstance. Somehow, they have not overpowered the golden threads though both have contributed to the weaving of our personal histories. Each thread has served to make of us the people who, by the grace of the Lord, will show how light will always overcome the darkness. The darker threads reveal the worth of the gold.'

'Manaen, beloved, the darker threads have, at times, threatened to control the warp and weft of our experience. It's wonderful how the prayer of faith can untangle the knots and straighten the strands. One thing more I will say of your Picture Parable: The Lord has bound our threads together. This has doubled the strength of the fabric. These threads will not fray!'

'Oh, Maryam, my dear, there are new threads to be woven into the cloth of our history that is yet to be written. It is our mutual desire to allow the gold of *Yeshua*–Jesus' choosing to give impetus to the weaving so that His workmanship will be discerned in the warp and weft of our worship and witnessing. With our faces to the "Son-Light", let's give Him today's threads for the on-going weaving of our tapestries, in prayer.

'Now, let's go to breakfast. Lydia, our "fabric friend", will be intrigued with this morning's Picture Parable. And my writing kit will have something to say as well—the story of the years.'

THE TAPESTRY OF LIFE

The tapestry of life
is woven by the threads
of long, eventful years
where light and shade are shed
upon the cloth that is prepared
in patterns sometimes rare:
an individual theme,
unique to circumstance!

The warp and weft of life
is wrought upon the loom
of human heritage
where colours glorious
entwine the light and shade,
the grey with gold, and weave
the pattern of God's will
beyond all remonstrance!

The pattern of one's life
is shaped by adroit Hands
beyond, yet in, our sphere.
The Lord of Light takes up
the threads we offer Him,
all frayed by frantic fears,
and He will knit them whole:
He has the governance!

(4) *The threads of red will tell*
of sacrifice—the Lord's!
The orange warmth is love;
the yellow: glowing joy.
The green holds vibrant life;
the blue, God's holiness.
The purple? For the King!
Here's Heaven's resonance!

And, what is life upon
this Earth without The Light
that casts His rays across
the fabric of our fragile faith
to show the threads of grace?
These hold the powerful form
of purpose in its place and has
eternal consequence!

The tapestry which speaks
of faithfulness through all
the windings of the way,
and holiness that weaves
integrity throughout,
displays abundant grace
which has, for those who see,
continuing pertinence!

APPENDIX

THE HEBREW ALPHABET—WITH "PICTURE PARABLES"

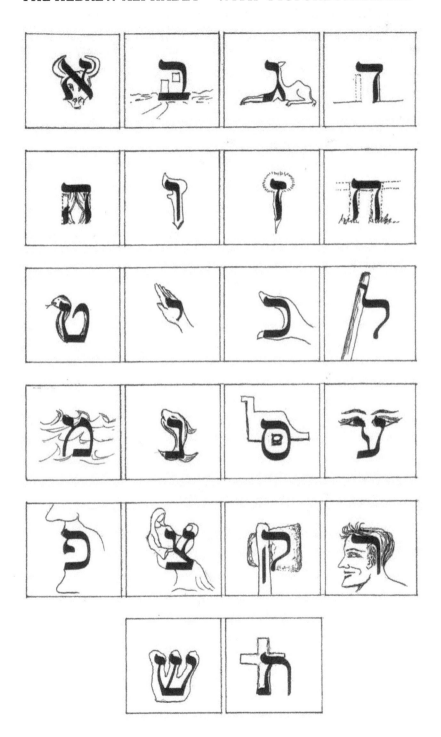

THE HEBREW ALPHABET
A guide to an alphabet's historical development

Ancient	Modern		Vocal	Variety	English
Ox head First	Paramount Powerful		aleph		A
Tent Open	House Family		beth	ע (final sound)	B
Foot Stable	Camel Walk		gimel	b.g.d.k.p.t. (. at centre: hard)	G
Entrance Access	Door Open		daleth	b.g.d.k.p.t. (soft: final)	D
Arms Upraised	Look Reveal		he		H
Tent peg Securing	Hook Held		vav	alt: waw	V, (W)
Seed Potential	Birth Heritage		zayin		Z
Wall Divide	Fence Company		heth	h: (throaty sound)	CH
Snake Alert	Serpent Danger		teth		(T)
Hand With arm	Work Worship		yodh		Y, I, J
Hand Open	Labour Action		kaph	ch (loch) (final)	K

Continued: THE HEBREW ALPHABET

Staff (Shepherd)	Teaching Learning	lamedh		L
Water (rough)	Water Chaotic	mem	(final placid)	M
Strength Endure	Fish Persist	nun	(final)	N
Aid Assist	Support Uphold	samekh	b.g.d.k.p.t. (soft: final)	(C)
Eye Sight	See Watch	ayin		(A)
Mouth Open	Mouth Face	pe,	ph (final) (final)	P, F
Trail Journey	Carry Assist	tsadhe	(final)	TS
Tool Work	Hammer/ Axe (cut)	qoph		Q
Head Control	Head Supreme	resh		R
Teeth Bite	Teeth Guard	sin/shin	. left top: s, . right top: sh	S
Sticks (crossed)	Mark Sign	tav,	th (final)	T

The distinct similarity between many of the most ancient Hebrew letters and the most modern English is remarkable, beyond coincidence! e.g. invert **A, d, m, n;** twist **b, c, q;** and **l, t,** remain as is.

PSALM 25

The classic example of a Hebraic acrostic poem

AN ALPHABET OF FAITH

Tune: *Come ye thankful people* 7.7.7.7. D.

A ll my life I dedicate,
B ravely place my trust in God!
C ome rejoice with me today;
D o not ever be disgraced:
E very soul should heed God's word,
F ollowing His disciplines.
G o along the path God set
H oping, trusting, voicing praise.

I have known unfailing love,
J ustice comes with circumstance:
K indness has revealed the way!
L ead me to the Truth You teach,
M indful You're the One who saved.
N ever blame me for my youth,
O nly know me in love's light:
P lease grant me Your healing touch.

Q uesting always to be true,
R escued from ensnaring foes,
S atisfied I'm in God's sight,
T rusting that the LORD will guide,
U tter joy invades my heart!
V ictory is my chief delight.
W onderful, His mercy now:
X claim, "God is at my side!"

....

Y onder are the joys of Heaven:
Z ealous, I will keep believing!

LLT

(Choir: chant the final two lines triumphantly)

Printed in Australia
AUHW020520040821
349787AU00001B/1